BERG

They framed him into prison.
He got out.

They beat him, cut him and tried to drown him.
They failed.

They tried to kill him as he lay helpless in a hospital bed.
They couldn't do it.

Then Bergman fought back. It meant taking on one of the most powerful gangs of the London underworld. He still fought . . . *his* way, in the dark from the shadows. He took their power and used it against them. All this during the dark days of 1940. The austerity of wartime, the terror of the blitz, form the sensationally visual backdrop to a taut compelling read.

Other books by Tom Barling
coming soon in Star:

THE SHOOTER MAN

BERGMAN'S BLITZ

Tom Barling

A STAR BOOK
published by
W. H. ALLEN

A STAR BOOK

Published in 1974
by W. H. Allen & Co. Ltd.
A division of Howard & Wyndham Ltd.
44, Hill Street, London W1X 8LB

First published in Great Britain by
W. H. Allen & Co. Ltd. 1973

Printed in Great Britain by
Richard Clay (The Chaucer Press) Ltd., Bungay, Suffolk

ISBN 0 352 30042 6

BERGMAN'S BLITZ

One

The early morning traffic choked Pentonville Road as I turned into it; stationary and honking at roadworks about a hundred yards on. One of the workmen was yelling Irish filth up into the cab of a Carter Patterson lorry, the others in the hole grinning and leaning on their picks.

The sky was a grey-blue haze, low and smelling of tar and woodsmoke. I breathed it in and it didn't hurt a bit. A crowd was gathering as the Carter Patterson driver waved his fist, yelling back.

I shoved through the crowd and brushed past a tall copper as he went forward reaching for his notebook. He said something and the navvy started explaining how he was only giving the poor fellow directions as he had lost his way. I could almost feel his mates nodding.

I cut across the traffic and ducked into the cool interior of a second-hand shop. It was filled from floor to ceiling with cupboards and sideboards, bedheads and tallboys. An old bloke with a headful of fluffy hair sat in the back room staring at a *Daily Mirror*, sucking his fingers over Jane. I wondered if she was putting them on or taking them off. I could see up the street in both directions.

The Carter Patterson lorry had pulled away and the navvies were genuflecting in their hole with the copper tucking his pencil away as though he had cleaned up the whole of the Smoke single-handed.

The traffic peeled off the queue and rolled towards King's Cross. A bus and a coach, a lorry, two more buses and then a long black saloon; two men in raincoats peering out at the pavements. The long arm reaching out for a quick look-see.

A bell rang in the back room and the old man breathed down my neck.

'Was there anything?' he asked in a thin voice, all gravy and no meat. I gave him a look at my teeth.

'It looked better through the window. I don't reckon it from a closer look.'

'Try Harrods,' he sneered. 'They're geared for the carriage trade.'

'Thanks, I'll think it over,' I said, and went out onto the street.

'Such a boaster,' he yelled after me, 'with what?'

I gave him another grin but he was already dinging through into his back room.

The black saloon was making a U-turn up ahead, the windows wound down. I kept on towards it, pretending not to notice. The face on my side ducked back as it passed me. It didn't do any good, the sun was in his eyes lighting him up like a Christmas tree. I'd have recognised that face anywhere. I let them pass me and roll on up to the roadworks where the oncoming stream had right of way, stopping them. Then I put my head down and ran like they do in the hot place.

I kept it up until I turned into the forecourt of King's Cross station. I bought a *Graphic* and caught my breath behind it. It was a slack time, between trains, and the cabs were sitting with their engines off in a shiny black line under the caked iron and glass canopy. The left luggage office was out of customers, the blokes behind the counter lolling and smoking. One of them had deep black sideburns running down into his blue chin. His eyes were sharp under his eyebrows, darting around at nothing and everything. I folded the paper and sauntered over to him.

He saw me and looked busily at his fingernails. I put

the parcel and the paper on the counter.

'Check this in for me, Sunshine,' I said.

He gave me a looking-over without his eyes catching mine.

'By the day or week?' he said in a sleepy way.

'The day.'

'There's no responsibility taken. It don't look too secure to me.'

'I'd have thought nicking my underwear would have been a bit above even a burke like you.' I matched him yawn for yawn.

'Mouthy,' he said, 'very mouthy.'

'That's me.'

He tore a ticket off his pad and stuck it onto the parcel, then flicked another with the same number on it at me.

'Fourpence,' he said.

'Daylight robbery,' I said.

'And you'd know, eh?'

We exchanged hard stares as I threw down the right money but it did neither of us any good. We'd both done too much of it in our time.

'Keep the paper, there's a lot of pictures in it,' I said. He put his hand on it and watched me walk away.

The Metropolitan line was a heaving mass of travellers as I passed the top of the stairs leading down onto the platforms. A train had just come in from Edgware way and the alighters were surging up the stairs. I quickened my pace and got to the Northern line concourse before they flowed around me. A neat little woman in the roller-front Bewlay's sold me a packet of Weights and a box of Swans. The crowd swilled away and I strolled back the way I'd come without meeting anybody, turning up the stairs to the Euston Road exit. I came up on the hot pavement across the road from the main line King's Cross station and stood for a while looking across at the back of the left luggage office. Trolleybuses passed, twittering as their poles crossed the wire junctions at the corner of Pancras Way. There were no black saloons in sight. I lit a Weight and sucked on it. The first tailor-made I'd tasted for a good long stretch. It tasted fine. Dryer than I remembered but fine.

A little fellow leaned against a lamp-post on the corner of Argyle Square. His face was set in a frown as he moved his lips over a folded *Greyhound Express.* He looked like he was picking losers with his tongue. His coat was too big and his trousers too short. A good two inches of sock showed over his lace-up boots. His cap had a broken brim. He yawned, showing long teeth with a lot of space between them. If a horse had teeth like it he'd have been first in the line for the knacker's yard.

I turned on my heel and went into the ABC café. Inside were a lot of deserted glass-topped tables, with the odd pensioner dotted about sipping tea and staring. I went along the self-service rail without picking up a tray. An old lady with matted grey hair pulled me up a cup of tea from the urn and rang twopence up on the till.

I sat down and stared along with the pensioners.

The little fellow with the broken brim came in and got himself a cup of tea. The till rang and he sat at a table to one side of me. He had shaved badly, little tufts of sandy hair sticking out all over his jaw. He stared out of the window as he stirred sugar into his tea, blowing on it without looking down.

'Got a light?' he said suddenly.

I dug the Swans out and handed them across without saying anything. He took a roll-up out of a tin and lit it up.

'Ta,' he said. He started to put the matches in his pocket.

'That's how I got 'em,' I said with my hand out.

'Third door on the right,' he said. 'The green one.' Then, 'Sorry, mate. Habit.'

He sucked his tea down in one and went off out into the street. I let a decent five minutes go by before I went back to the left luggage office. The bloke with the busy eyes and the slow face was taking a couple of cases in from a fussy matron that talked like she caught buses but thought Rolls Royce. She was telling him not to scuff them as they were new and a present from her brother in Cambridge. A professor, no less. The bloke slapped on the labels as though he was thumbing flies.

'I'll want the right money, missus,' he said. 'No change.'

'Really,' said the matron, raking through a handbag big enough to keep plumber's tools in. After a lot of muttering and rattling she managed the right coins.

'Thank *you*, madam,' said Slowface. She scooped up the tickets and clattered off towards platform two. Slowface took up the cases from the counter and carried them to the nearest clear space in the rack, throwing them in with all the force he could muster. His mouth flickered into a brief smile.

I took out my ticket and held it out to him. His eyes danced all around it.

'Yes, so soon,' I said, saving him from thinking of something witty. He leered over my shoulder as someone came up behind me and took hold of my wrist.

I looked at Slowface and he looked at me and the bloke holding my arm walked around to the side of me and flashed his warrant card.

'Withdrawal, Bergman?' he said in his medium copper's voice. I looked at him then, seeing Slowface start to make himself scarce.

'Don't go away,' said the copper.

He was medium height, about five-eight in a three-quarter length blue mac and size nine shoes. His shirt was light blue and his tie thin and black. I couldn't see his socks but I'd have bet they were black too. His face was slightly boiled pink, scrubbed looking, with eyes like buffed buttons. His sideburns were brown under his charcoal trilby. The warrant card said his name was Barrett J.G. and that he was a Det. Serg. out of King's Cross Road Station.

'Where'd you steal that?' I said for something to say.

He ignored that.

'Give him his parcel,' he said to Slowface. Slowface shrugged and walked off through the racks. Without looking round I knew there was another one behind me. He was making the kind of noises people make when they're trying to breathe softly. We all waited until my parcel was plonked on the counter.

'Shall I open it up?' I said. Barrett smiled, showing some gum.

'Saves time,' he said.

I pulled the knot loose, tumbling the gear. Barrett eyed it without using his hands. He looked like he wanted to hold his nose.

'Satisfied?' I said.

Barrett shrugged. It was something for his shoulders to do while he gave himself a headache thinking. There was a creak of raincoat as the man behind me made a gesture. Barrett turned to Slowface.

'Anything else of his in there?'

'How would I know? If he's got a ticket then he's got a parcel. If he hasn't, he hasn't.'

'Not bright, are you?' said Barrett.

'If I was I wouldn't be here. That stands to reason. Next you'll be asking do I remember seeing him bring this one in. Did I take it in? Well I don't. I never do.'

I swallowed and waited.

'Have you got another ticket?' Barrett asked.

'Me?' I said.

'You,' he said.

'No,' I said.

There was a pause. A train let off steam in a long hiss

and the pigeons took to the air to do their obligatory circuit of the rafters. The newsvendor yelled that he had the first editions of the evening papers and a couple of travellers banged taxi doors.

'You can go through my pockets if you want,' I offered. Barrett looked like he wanted to but something he was reading in the face behind me stopped him. He shrugged again. He was a good shrugger.

'Do up your parcel,' he said. 'There's clean air getting inside.'

'Yes, Mister Barrett,' I said and got the parcel back into shape.

'Hey,' said Slowface. 'The ticket.'

I gave him the ticket and he jammed it on a metal spike.

'Hey,' he said again.

Barrett watched him hand me the *Graphic*.

'You forgot your paper,' he said.

'Thanks.'

He walked back into the racks without another word.

Barrett and the other man followed me out of the station right up to the entrance of the Underground. I went down the steps and looked back when I got to the bottom. They had gone.

Two

The third door on the right up Argyle Square was green. Just. The latest topcoat had cracked and faded and a lot of it had fallen away, letting the previous brown show through in rusty streaks. It was a three-storey building with bad pointing and large windows, all of them dirty, some of them cracked. The ones either side of the front door had No Vacancy signs in them. They had been there a long time, long enough to yellow and mottle with flydirt. Black lettering on the window above the door said: Argyle House. The g and s were just putty outlines on the glass.

I pressed the bell and waited. Nothing happened so I pressed it again, with my ear up against the door. Nothing. No ring or buzz or chime. I heaved on the lion-head knocker and made echoes inside. A door creaked and slammed and shoes clacked on lino. A bolt was thrown, then a chain rattled.

The door swung in about an inch, maybe an inch and a half. The little man from the ABC shoved most of his nose through the opening.

'Rent man,' I said, 'and you're three weeks behind. No promises—just cash.'

'Hang on,' said the little man. He closed the door to let off the chain, taking his time. I kicked the bottom rail, loosening more of the paint.

'Come on, Ernie. For fuck's sake.'

'All right, all right,' he said. 'Come ahead.'

The hall was brown. Brown paintwork, brown lino, brown rose wallpaper. The hallstand and the letter-board were mahogany. Stairs to the left led to the upper floors and a short flight led down to the basement. Ernie thumbed towards the down flight.

'How are you, boy?' said Ernie. He gripped me around the waist for an instant with surprising strength. A taller man would have thrown his arm around my shoulder. I slapped him on the back.

'Fine, considering.'

'Been a long time.'

'For you and me both.'

We nodded at each other for a bit before I followed him down the stairs. Ernie tapped on a half-glazed door that borrowed light from nowhere.

'Come in,' said a strong old voice, harsh and feminine. It belonged to an old biddy sitting in a high-back rocker. I could only see her as an outline before my eyes adjusted to the gloom.

'Here he is then,' said Ernie.

A hand came forward, the outstretched fingers covered in a shopful of rings, the nails crimson. I took it and we shook hands like men. Her skin was as dry and warm as an adder's belly. I felt I could have struck matches on her palm.

'Sit yourself down, Mister Bergman,' she said. 'Ernie, pour him a drink.'

'Gin, Bergie?'

'If that's what's going.'

'That's what's going,' said the woman and made a sound in her throat like stones rattling in a well. She would have called it laughing.

I could see better. The room was bigger than I'd thought at first. There was a grand piano with the lid closed in front of the half-drawn curtains. A twenties-looking silk square with tasselled edges was draped over the top, a little city of framed pictures grouped in streets hiding most of the pattern. Ernie was rattling a bottle of Gordon's against a tumbler by a sideboard.

The top of that was covered with bottles. I've seen boozers with less stock.

The walls were a patchwork of playbills and music hall posters with most of the greats listed. There was Marie Lloyd beside George Robey, Little Tich under Dan Leno, and Billy Bennet watching Harry Lauder keeping right on to the end of the road. Marie Dresden and Dame Sarah Bernhardt looked out of place between a tumbling act and smiling Max Miller. They were all autographed *'to Dotty Claire with love'*. It didn't take a genius to work out who Dotty Claire was.

She sat with her sparkling fingers wrapped around a tall glass, gently working the rocker. Her face was thin and her neck slender, still elegant despite the cording of age and the deep salt cellars. Her eyebrows were drawn in surprised curves over deep-lidded luminous eyes, the pupils washed-out blue. Her mouth was painted in a cupid's bow the red of her nails. Her dress was black and long with puffed sleeves. Her hair was a mess of piled-up streaky grey. She was more eighteen ninety than nineteen thirty-nine.

Ernie handed me the drink.

'You do like it neat?' asked Dotty Claire.

'I do now,' I said. I took a good bite of it and listened to it run down onto my prison breakfast. I looked at Ernie, who grinned, and at Dotty Claire, who didn't.

'I've told the Duchess all about you,' said Ernie. 'I knew you wouldn't mind.'

'Did you.'

'Yeah, she was right interested. Reckon she could help out if you'd a mind. You know?'

'Do I?'

'Well, yeah.'

Dotty rattled more stones.

'Oh, he minds. He minds a lot,' she said. 'Like mad he minds.'

'I mind,' I agreed. My voice came out as thick as

navvies' tar. The gin and the porage growled at each other so I took sides and swallowed some more.

Dotty's heels pecked at the floor as she brought the rocker to a halt and leaned forward. Her nose was less than a foot from mine.

'Why not?' she said. 'Why no help?'

'I like being on my ownsome. It saves sweat.'

'Not what you've got in mind doesn't.'

'Just change the money, Duchess. The usual ten per cent. That way we both make. Then I'll be on my way.'

I threw the *Graphic* at Ernie.

'It should all be there.'

He leafed through from the headlines to the sports pages, sliding fivers out in thin bundles, stacking them on his knee.

'That's the whole four hundred. Any sweat getting it?' he said.

'The local law watched Ronny give it to me. Bloke called Barrett flashed his warrant at me. Gave me a free escort up the road with it, as it happens.'

'Barrett,' sneered Ernie, 'the terror of the tarts. Got 'em all on a rota round here. You this week, Rosie. Next week Linda. Pay the fine and wave it around for another trouble-free month. I'll be round on Friday for a packet of fags. Oh, what a surprise, there's a tenner in the lining, I wonder how that got there.'

'Yeah, he frightened the life out of me,' I said.

Dotty stripped a note off the top of the pile and held it up to the light coming through the curtains, turning it and fingering the paper.

'It's a right one,' she said. 'Why change 'em up?'

I sighed.

'Because although they're paying me off for the time, they don't want me about, right? They should be hot enough to burn your fingers.'

She squinted at me over the top of a second note, nodding slowly.

'Give me the numbers book, Ernie,' she said. Ernie pulled a pad of printed sheets out of the sideboard. Dotty riffled the pages, stopped, and ran her fingers down the page.

'House,' she said. 'The Baker Street Lloyd's last month. Twelve thousand over the counter in fives and ones.'

'That's about it,' I said.

'So you get stopped with a pocketful by the law and it's "Try explaining how you got hold of these" down at the nick. The bastards.'

'Not too clever,' I said.

Dolly made a nasty sound in her throat to match her feelings. 'Nice friends to have,' she said.

'Not my choice, Ernie's. I tried telling him.'

Ernie's mouth got white and pinched and he shredded the roll-up he was holding between his fingers. 'And you got the stretch,' he said. 'As Gawd is my judge, that was the last thing, the very last, straight.'

'Who's reminding?' I said.

'How do you want it?' asked Dotty.

'Half-quid notes. Make two equal bundles, keep one here and I'll take one with me. Take anything Ernie owes out of the half you keep.'

'Not much change there,' she said. 'But there's other things more important to discuss.'

'Like what?'

'Like, what now for you?'

'I'll make out.'

'Stop it, Bergman, you're giving me a pain in the corset. The great I Am. Giant the Jack Killer. You won't get six feet without help.'

'Listen to her, Bergie. Just listen.'

I kept my eyes on my gin.

'You can't charge out of here and go after a copper you think is bent, not being marked the way you are. The boys aren't going to take kindly to you being loose either. Especially when they know you've sussed the snide gelt. Stay low, let it cool down. Give it three months—four, maybe, then...'

She started rocking again, jerky and rapid.

'Half time,' said Ernie, 'bring out the lemons.'

I couldn't think of a thing to say. I just looked at the carpet through the bottom of my glass. As the level went down the carpet got clearer.

'He's a fool, Ernie,' Dotty rasped. 'A bloody mental cripple, going after West End pros just for doing a two-stretch on dodgy evidence. He can't even walk down the street without getting run in for being sober in charge of a pair of boots.'

'Finished?' I said.

'Not by half,' she said.

I stood up.

'Yes you have. Let's have it.' I held my hand out for the money. She picked a black patent bag up from beside her chair and pulled bundles of money out, throwing me a couple. There must have been thousands in there.

'You should keep that in a bank,' I said.

She gave me an irritated look. 'That's where it was before I got it,' she snarled. 'And don't get hungry-looking either. It wouldn't do you any good.' She held out a cocked automatic, one of those sheathed Yankee jobs. 'I've shot more than apples off people's heads with this.'

I held up my hands and threw her the worried look she seemed to expect.

'Thanks for the drink,' I said. 'See you around, Ern.'

'But,' said Ernie, 'but I thought I was going, like with you.'

'Shows how wrong you can be, doesn't it? Teddah,' I said and let myself out.

The sun was directly overhead when I got back on the street, the traffic was building up for the lunchtime jam.

A slow horse pulling a junk cart clopped past with its nose deep in its feedbag. The driver looked asleep. Two little girls were skipping with a rope tied to a lamp-post, chanting:

'One potato, two potatoes, three potatoes, four.'

Their mums were gossiping across the area railings, not bothering to keep their voices down. Up in the centre square where a bunch of dispirited elms stood on the raw earth, an old man shuffled along with the aid of a heavy stick. Sun glinted on his war medals. The way things were going he might get a chance to go back to France again. He didn't look anxious about it.

I turned down towards Euston Road and saw a bloke ease out of a rooming house across the way folding a paper. He yawned as he came down the steps to give himself a casual look. He crossed the road and fell in behind me.

I got to the corner and turned round suddenly to walk in quick strides back to him. He looked startled despite himself.

'Time,' I said.

'What?' he said, taking a side-step.

'The time, what is it?'

'Oh,' he looked down at his wrist, 'quarter past twelve.'

'That'll give you something to write in your notebook.'

'I don't...' he said.

'Twelve fifteen. Bergman asked me the time. Evidence.'

He looked lost for words, little sweat beads popping onto his top lip. I gave him a hard look until he crossed the road again and hurried off in the direction of Warren Street. I stayed where I was until he had stopped looking over his shoulder and decided to keep walking. Copper or nark, it didn't matter, he was bloody inept.

I crossed the junction of Gray's Inn Road and where York Way empties out into the bottom of Pentonville

Road. It was only a minute's walk to King's Cross Road from there. The cinema on the corner was showing a George Formby and an old Western with Hoot Gibson in it. Not one I'd bother with. I walked on until I got to the little boozer that lays back on the right. The doors were open and the smell of old ale was right across the pavement. I went in and ordered up a half of Burton, my eyes on the door. I'd just taken the foam off the top by the time Ernie came past.

'Pull us another one, guv,' I said. Two strides and I had Ernie's collar, pulling him into the bar.

'You're pinched,' I said.

'Oh, Bergie,' he said. 'What a surprise.'

'Balls. Drink your beer.'

'Oh,' he said. 'Yeah. Ta.'

'I'm not paying for it, you bloody toerag. You are.'

'Oh, yeah. Well, yeah,' he said digging into his pocket and hopping about as if he had a bootful of hot splinters. He spilled coins onto the counter and the bloke behind the bar scooped up enough, leaving him a lonely penny on the mahogany. Ernie whipped it off the bar as if it was a newly minted sovereign. It went into his pocket with a roar like a butterfly with croup. He'd got the glass to his mouth when I grabbed his arm. Beer spilled down his waistcoat.

''Ere,' he said.

'Where, I mean, just where were you going?' I said.

The till pinged thoughtfully. Ernie's mouth went down at the corners, he swallowed and moved his neck inside his collar.

'Walk. That's all. A walk.'

'Thirsty-making, walking is.'

'Yeah,' said Ernie, his eyes watchful, 'yeah.'

'You're thirsty then?'

'Never say no to a drink, Bergie. You know that.'

I could see his mind working behind his eyebrows. He hunched over to sniff in some beer.

'And it's a celebration, sort of,' he said. 'You back again and all. Cheers.'

I let go of his arm and rapped on the bar.

'Guv, give us four pints. With handles.'

The bloke stayed where he was by the till until I peeled a ten-bob note off my roll. They were the fastest pints I've ever seen pulled. He rang up the till and brought me the change. I pointed at Ernie.

'They're for him,' I said, shoving the change back across the bar. 'See he drinks them before he leaves.'

He nodded without cracking a smile. Ernie didn't look well.

'See you in half an hour, Ern,' I said. 'Be here.'

He watched me walk out with his elbow in among the mugs.

Three

King's Cross Road Police Station was a four-storey building built of grey Victorian brick, right next door to the court. It had windows with elegant Georgian proportions and a film of dust on them. It had a central entrance underneath and a white-stone carved lion and unicorn holding the royal arms between them as they sat on a motto. Below *Dieu Et Mon Droit* somebody had carved *Police Station* over the door and just behind the iron rail that the blue lamp hung from. There were heavy railings around some scruffy grass on either side of the narrow path that led up to the double doors at the top of four steps. I walked along the path and up the steps and pushed through the doors.

The desk sergeant was behind a counter that had a two-tone finish; mahogany and fagburns. He looked up as the doors closed with a grind and a snap. He gave me a cursory glance before dropping his eyes to the register, his pen scratching busily.

With that one shot he had summed me up; a scruffbag looking for directions to Rowton House for a doss and a bowl of soup.

'Up on the right before the first set of lights,' he said, with his head down. 'If you've the three-ha'pence.'

I leaned on his counter and looked at the posters and circulars on the notice-board behind him. The usual dog-eared selection of stolen jewellery, silver and plate, a couple of men wanted with long descriptions that could fit nobody and anybody, a recruiting poster for the force, and one for the armed services. Right at the bottom was a red ink reminder to turn off the lights in unused offices.

'Barrett in?' I said to the top of his head.

He sighed and put his pen down across an unused ashtray and straightened up to give me a longer second look.

'You mean *Mister* Barrett, don't you?'

'I suppose I do.'

He let his lids down over his pupils instead of nodding, saving his energy for something more important.

'Take a seat and I'll see.'

I looked at the row of hard chairs and shook my head.

'Not with my delicate constitution. Either you're interested in some snide or you're not. Are you?'

He picked up his pen and put it down again.

'Your name, sir?' he asked. The 'sir' cost him a lot.

I told him and something flicked in his eyes, a slight squirm in the hazel depths. He didn't pull his hair or roll on the floor or even spit. He wrote my name in the book with the time and date, leaving all the other columns blank in the section he had allotted me, raised the counter flap and beckoned me down the passage that led to a stair-well. We went up the first flight and along another passage past doors where conversation buzzed and typewriters clacked. We stopped outside a door with a blank card in the slot and he used his knuckles.

'Come,' said a medium voice.

The sergeant tucked his head round the door and said something I couldn't catch. There was a pause. A chair scraped and the door opened all the way.

'In here, you,' Barrett said to me. 'Thanks, Tom,' he said to the sergeant.

I slid past him and came up short with my knees up against the sides of two desks that faced each other, leaving just enough room for two chairs, a filing cabinet and a wastepaper basket. Barrett sat in his chair and shook his head at the man sitting behind the other desk. The other man shook his head too. I just stood there, pretending nervous patience. After a bit they looked across at me with blank faces.

The other man was a lot bigger than Barrett, fleshier, and, from the way his legs doubled back under his chair, taller too. He had freckles on the top of his head instead of hair, eggshell brown against the pink skin. His eyes were quiet under heavy eyebrows and his firm mouth clamped down on the stem of a yellow-wood pipe.

I threw my bundle of notes on the table between them. Only their eyes moved.

'I was worried about these, so I thought, well...' I let the words trail away. Nobody said anything. The clock on the wall ticked with military precision and the calendar under it told us yesterday's date. I reached out my Weights and fumbled one alight. Barrett looked at the other man, looked at me, and we all looked at the money.

'Worried,' said Barrett, so quietly that I almost thought I'd imagined it. Then, 'He was worried about the money.'

'Was he?' said the other man.

'That's what he said. Worried.'

'Yeah, well somebody owed me that. Gave it me, and I thought if I wasn't careful. You know how it is, there's a lot of dodgy characters about. So if you'd look it over for me.'

I sounded stupid even to me. Barrett picked up the wad and flicked through it, flicked through again and threw it to the other man.

'What do you think then, Mister Parsons? A lag with the porage still wet on his lips coming in here with enough dough to choke a stable full of ponies is worried. Wouldn't you like worries like that? Wouldn't you like it more than putting your flat feet up with a thin retirement pension? A few bob to help keep the cold out.'

Parsons riffled the notes under his nose, breathing in a slow breath, one hand over his freckles.

'I've got a greenhouse,' he said. 'Keep dahlias. There's a lot of corms in this bundle. Maybe a new house, all glass with a metal frame and crazy-paving all round it.'

'An army of garden gnomes,' said Barrett.

'Not partial to gnomes,' said Parsons with his nose in the money. 'There's too many in the cells for me to want any in my garden.'

Barrett grinned without showing his teeth. He said: 'Empty your pockets.'

'But look, Mister Barrett, I came in in good faith. All I want is to see them notes is square. I thought I'd come to the law and play it straight. I didn't reckon on being turned over. Straight I didn't,' I said with my hands in my pockets and the Weight in one corner of my mouth.

Barrett got up fast and was breathing into the side of my neck before I could blink. There wasn't really enough room for him to do anything physical. I kept my eyes on Parsons.

'You cheeky burke,' said Barrett. 'Come off it. You wouldn't know we'd had an anonymous on the blower about you, would you? You just walked in without knowing a bloody thing. Dewy-eyed. I could puke.'

Parsons looked pained. 'Barrett, lad. Don't let him get your goat. He's sussed the bubble was out, that's all. You win some, you lose some. This is a hung decision. Nothing's changed. Sit down. Light up, there's a lot of day left.'

Barrett did some heavy breathing into my ear before he flopped back into his chair. Parsons opened his drawer and skimmed twenty Gold Flake into Barrett's lap. Barrett used a gold lighter to light up, forcing smoke through his nostrils. His colour stayed high, almost purple around his eyes. Parsons held the money out at arm's length.

'Take it, lad,' he said. 'I could hold you for thirty-six hours. I could have you helping police with their enquiries. There's a lot I *could* do. A lot. A bright lad like you would know that. An hour in and an hour out. Could keep it up for weeks. Wearing on the nerves, is that. I've known hardheads cry over it. Confess to murdering themselves to get some rest, they would. Seen them all.'

I put out my hand and the money flopped into it. Barrett spat tobacco flecks onto his blotter and stared out of the window. There was a long sullen silence, even the traffic stopped. Parsons moved his pipe to the other side of his mouth and moved the papers around on his desk with even strokes of his hands. He made three piles, lifting each to square them with sharp taps.

'Go away, lad,' he said in a tired voice. 'You're just another pile of paperwork to me.'

'Thank you, Mister Parsons,' I said. 'You've lifted a weight off, I can tell you. I won't forget it. Straight.'

'Piss off,' he said, waving me out of the door. 'Don't compound the felony with baldfaced balls.'

I went out quick and closed the door without more than a click. The desk sergeant was laying the internal phone in its cradle as I went past him. He gave me a humourless smile and noted the time in his register.

Book them in, book them out, never forget a face. The law all over.

There were a few people in the bar now, the lunch-time drinkers, slow pint men, easing the ache of the morning out of their bones. Quiet men with no conversation, heavy in their chairs with their eyes focussed middle-distance. Ernie was on his last pint, draped over the bar with his eyes on the door, mouth open.

I snapped my fingers for one of the same and watched the pump being worked. My feet ached and the back of my head felt tight and slightly hot. I'd have given a pound for a good night's kip. Ernie was working up to a sulk. Now I was back he could feel aggrieved. It wouldn't do him any good, the mood I was in.

'He's done well,' said the bloke behind the bar, 'supping like a good'un.'

'Threatening bastard made me,' said Ernie.

'Have one yourself, guv,' I offered. He blinked no with his mouth closed and took the money off up to the till.

'Drink up, Ern. There's a long day ahead. A lot to do,' I said, taking a long swallow. It was good ale, from the wood, with the smoky taste of oak. Six pints of it and you were armour-plated. Two more and the bolts stuck in you.

'Are you in a fit state to listen?' I asked. Ernie almost pulled himself upright, elbows hard in at his sides. He bobbed his head carefully, trying not to spill anything. Trying hard.

'Anything you want?' he said.

'A driving job. Kept in practice, have you?'

Ernie was one of the best coachmen on wheels in the Home Counties. When he took the wheel of a motor it would do just about anything but back-flips at ninety through a row of back gardens. He could drive under a bus without getting his ticket punched, picking the conductor's pocket on the way.

'I've kept loose.'

'Glad to hear it.'

'When for?'

'Tonight, could be.'

'It wouldn't be tonight definitely, would it?'

'On the cards.'

Ernie's face set itself in careful planes as he got on top of the ale, giving himself room to think.

'What's on?'

'On?' I said.

'That's not all I get to know if I'm in on a tickle. You told me never go in blind.'

'That's with strangers. What you don't know you can't bleat.'

'I dunno,' he said.

I just looked at him. He dropped his gaze and made squiggles in a pool of beer on the bar with his little finger. I sank the rest of my pint and clicked the glass down close to his hand. The barman looked but I waved him off.

'Teddah then, Ern.'

'Hold up, bloody hang on.'

'What, for nothing? Not me.'

I started out of the door.

'All right,' he said.

I kept on and out onto the pavement towards the Cross. He caught me up a few strides on, double-stepping to keep pace.

'Listen, can't you. I said all right.'

I stopped suddenly and he had to turn back to face me. I patted his cheek.

'Then you're in,' I said.

'All right. I said so. Blimey, you ain't half got moody since you come out.'

'Six o'clock in the Ship. If I don't show have yourself a night out. And don't sit with your nose half out of the door, right?'

'Right,' he said. 'What about the wheels?'

'I'll get that squared.'

I crossed the road leaving him where he stood. Poor ugly little burke. But that was the way it had to be.

The phone burred a dozen doubles before the receiver was lifted. I pressed button A and the coins dropped.

'Left luggage. Hello.'

'Let me have Ronny.'

'Who wants him? This a private call? It ain't allowed on the company phone.'

'Station Master's office. There's a query on his cards.'

'Oh, sorry sir. Just being careful.'

'Very commendable,' I said.

The phone scraped on wood as it was put down. I

listened to cases being humped and stacked, voices fuzzing, and the distant rattle of trolleys. There was obviously a train in.

'Hello,' said Ronnie.

'Thought you'd like to know you passed Bergman snide,' I said.

Ronny made a noise in his throat.

'Who's this?'

'Does it matter, son? Bergman knows too. I don't think he's pleased. Well, he wouldn't be, would he?'

'Who's this talking? You a friend of his?'

'More than you are, it looks like.'

'Listen,' said Ronny in a hurry, 'I don't know nothing from nothing. If you're with the passers or a friend of the bloke it was passed to, the message is the same. I didn't know, right. If you're with the first lot, then step off the pavement if you see me. That's a real shit-trick. If you know Bergman, tell him the same. What a bastard stroke to pull. Jesus.'

'I'll pass the message,' I said. 'I hope you know which side your bread's buttered.'

'Both sides,' spat Ronny. 'Come round and I'll butter yours.'

He slammed the phone down and left me with an earful of silence. I put the receiver down carefully and slid the doors of the booth open to let the bustle of the Underground in and the cigarette smoke out.

'You finished?' said a bloke with one eye on his watch.

I stepped out and let him slide in to push his pennies in the slot.

'I hope she's worth it,' I said through the closing doors. He gave me a look black with promise before turning to dial. I went up the stairs to the entrance up inside the suburban line station and walked round to where I could watch the front of the left luggage office.

The concourse was packed. People swarmed everywhere, humping cases and dragging kids, yelling for porters and avoiding the taxis. Late holiday-makers, most of them, off to suck in some sunshine in the northern resorts. I reckoned they were going in the wrong direction.

The queue for luggage was a long crocodile with its tail in York Way. The boys were frantic behind the counter. I saw Ronny arguing with one of the others as he shrugged into his topcoat. The bloke said something that Ronny didn't like because he spat on the floor and banged out through the side door the big trolleys use.

I dodged back round the buttress and waited for him to pass me.

There was a bang, a squeal of brakes and a lot of confused yelling. A taxi came round past me in a slide, its motor roaring. I caught sight of a face behind the wheel, heavy-featured and unshaven. Then the cab was past me and round through the forecourt of the Great Northern Hotel. Its nearside wheel hit a pile of cases stacked at the bottom of the steps, exploding them. The porter and a middle-aged couple went over in a heap with the clothing flying around them.

I felt my stomach turn over as I scrambled round into the concourse. The queue had broken ranks and was a jostling ring around something on the ground. I forced my way through the outer fringes and right to the centre. Ronny lay on his back with one leg doubled up under him at an impossible angle. His quick eyes were open but fixed on a distant cloud, blood bubbling from his nose. He looked white and calm. I got down beside him and ripped off his tie, fumbling with his shirt buttons.

He turned his head enough to look at me, smiling with broken teeth.

'I didn't know,' he said, soft as soap.

I put my head down close.

'I know it, son. They won't have the last word on this, straight.'

'I know,' he murmured, 'that's good to...'

He closed his eyes and went to sleep.

The crowd rippled behind me and somebody's knee took me in the back, a hand gripped my shoulder, steadying itself. I shrugged it off.

'Get back off me, you clocking bastards. Seen enough, have you?'

Feet shuffled and the ring of feet widened.

'He just walked straight out in front of him. I saw it,' said a woman.

'He didn't stop though, did he? Looked deliberate,' said somebody else. Muttered conversations broke out.

Heavy boots stepped into the space the other side of Ronny's body.

'Stand back there. Give him air,' said the copper. 'Has somebody phoned for an ambulance?'

'In the left luggage. They phoned from there,' said a man's voice.

'Right,' said the copper.

I stood up and back. The copper stepped round the widening circle, pushing me back with everybody else. It suited. There was nothing I could do for him. I went out through the crowd and away quickly without hurrying. I wasn't tired any more.

Four

I dropped off the bus before it finally ground to a halt. The conductor leaned round the handrail and rang the bell. The bus swung out through the lights on amber, carved up a lorry and turned right.

The afternoon was dying fast as rain clouds scudded over the buildings, banking and rolling in the warm wind. It was hot and sticky, the sort of heat you only get in a city in July. I walked past a huddle of scruffy shops and a closed pub, a furniture warehouse and a church with scaffolding up around its spire. A couple of workmen were lowering roof slates in a wicker basket to a man on the ground. They weren't hurrying.

I cut across a side street and onto the forecourt of a garage with a deep, high concrete canopy over the pumps. A pantechnicon and two lorries stood under the canopy, half concealing the aerodrome-type sliding doors. I squeezed past them to the gap that led to the office.

'Who'd you want?' somebody said.

A young bloke sat behind the wheel of the pantechnicon, the window slid back as he stared at me. His hair was up in an elaborate quiff over his round face, his eyes were dull brown and he had spots.

'Well?' he said.

'Talking to me?' I said back.

'Who'd y'think?'

I held on to what temper I had left and carefully said: 'Cliff. Is he around?'

The boy moved his shoulders against the back-rest as he opened a packet of Wrigley's.

'That depends, don't it?' he said around the stick of gum.

'On what?'

'On who's asking.'

'I'm asking.'

He gave me the tough, insolent sort of look that takes hours of practice in the mirror when your mum's not looking.

'Well,' he said, 'I don't know who you are, do I? And if I don't know, it still depends, don't it?'

I watched him chew his gum for a bit before saying anything else. Somebody was spot-welding out the back somewhere, and somebody else was hitting a metal sheet. It was an odd mixture of sounds. The kid chewed his gum and I ran out of patience.

'Tell him I was in,' I said. 'I'll be back next week with the hundred.'

He leaned out of the window, his head and neck clear of the glass.

'Hundred? Hundred what?' he asked.

I just looked at him.

'Well,' he said, 'if it's money, I'll take care of it. Cliff leaves all that to me.'

'Right-hand man, eh?'

'Yeah.'

He stuck his arm out with the palm uppermost.

'I'll cop for him,' he said.

I took hold of his hand and twisted it a hundred and eighty degrees. His head and neck turned upside down and his legs came into sight, thrashing against the windscreen. I took a step forward and pressed his arm against the door of the cab. His legs went straight out and his face turned a funny colour. His left foot banged against the centre of the steering wheel, hit the horn and stayed there. Now there were three interesting sounds. Four, if you counted his breathing as he tried to keep the contents of his stomach.

After a bit the hammer stopped banging, the torch was turned off and footsteps made echoes along with a lot of grumbling.

'Sid! What are you doing, boy? What's that with the horn?'

Sid stayed on his back, concentrating on his breathing.

'Out here, Cliff,' I said.

A tall, stooped Negro came out of the garage, blinking in the sunshine. His hair was as white as his eyeballs. His flat nose was flatter than it should have been, ridged with coffee-coloured scar tissue. His hands and wrists hung a long way below the cuffs of his boiler suit. He looked at Sid, then at me, then back at Sid.

'You playing havoc with that battery, boy,' he said. 'Hello, Bergie.' He leaned sideways against the wall and fished out an Old Holborn tin, taking his time rolling a cigarette.

'That boy give you some stick then, Bergie boy? I wouldn't be s'prised.'

I nodded.

'Still,' said Cliff, 'you let him go now, maybe. He looks dumb-animal sick.'

I let go of Sid's arm. It swung up to twelve o'clock as he fell down onto the floor of the cab. The horn stopped and it went very quiet. I threw Cliff my Swans and he lit up.

'You was quick coming to see me. Only this morning I hear you was out,' Cliff said in a cloud of smoke.

'You heard right,' I said. 'Office still in the same place?'

'It is.'

He lobbed me my matches and I followed him through the crack in the doors. Inside was twilight. We threaded past a row of confectioner's vans, a saloon half way through a respray and a red sports up on blocks next to a double row of oil drums. Cliff opened a sliding door and clicked on a forty-watt bulb.

The office was about eight feet square with a bare

concrete floor and layers of thick felt on the walls and ceiling. There was a scarred desk with a phone and a film of dust, a swivel chair, an armchair against the wall and two filing cabinets. There were no windows. Cliff perched on the desk and I sat in the armchair. Without moving his feet he opened the top drawer of the nearest file and came up with a bottle of Haig. I shook my head and he up-ended the bottle into his mouth. It stayed up a long time. He had a swallow like the first night of shore leave.

He sighed, smacked his lips and kissed the label.

'What you need, boy?'

'The wheels I left with you, if you've kept them sweet.'

'As a nut. That car could win at Goodwood tomorrow.'

I reached for my roll and said: 'What's the damage?'

Cliff held up his hand.

'Nothing this trip, boy. There'll be times coming up when you'll do me something. That right?'

'Couldn't be righter. Keep the shooters under wraps but close. I don't see any use for 'em straight off, but then it's a hard old game.'

Cliff rolled the bottle into its drawer, said goodbye to it and locked it up. His roll-up had gone out and he spent some time pinching off the dead ash.

'I been hearing some bubbles, Bergie. Nothing straight, you know. But there's a lot of dog-ends come in here. Put 'em together, you get yourself a whole smoke.'

He scratched his chin, then his cheek, then pulled the lobe of his ear.

'Let's have it, then, Cliff. I know you still garage for Spanner's mob. That's good business. You know it doesn't keep me awake at night. We've been friends for too long. Just tell me without the chat, I'm running on borrowed time. Where's Laurie? I just want that bastard, nothing else can get up my nose. Just him.'

'That's the pin in the winkle, boy. He ain't solo no more. He's done a deal with Spanner. Top boy round there now. He was just waiting for the chance. Done more praying than cathedral full of bishops.'

I took the last Weight out and rolled it in my fingers, tapping it on my packet. It made sense. Laurie always was one for crowds. I crumpled the packet and threw it onto the desk. It skidded along the top and swept off the other side onto the floor.

'I still want him, Cliff. The only thing that's changed is how careful I've got to be. That's all.'

Cliff was half way to the floor with his hand out for the cigarette packet. He froze with his fingers spread.

'Sheet,' he said, 'that's all? You couldn't be that careful if you was house-trained in a palace. That's the Spandrell mob you talking about. What you want? You want to get killed six times a week and twice on Sundays? It ain't just you, you know. There's others going to get tied up in this. You got to think of your friends, man. That too hard for you to do?'

I felt as quiet as a sink with the plug pulled. I put the fag in my mouth and got it alight.

'Friends like you, Cliff?' I said as softly as I could.

His face went almost green as he straightened up, curling his fingers under the lip of the desk. His knuckles went yellow.

'That's a black thing to say, boy. No excuse for that. No excuse. I never asked you for a thing before. We was friends from that time in the docks. Maybe you need reminding of that.'

'No,' I said. 'Don't even think it.'

'Well,' he said, 'it's gonna get said all the same. I was down that night when they was all round me with chains and bricks. They knew I wouldn't throw that fight, but they wanted a good bet. I would have been the contender, left alone. That manager was made of cream cheese, telling them I'd go to sleep in the fifth for a handful of money.'

'Ancient history, Cliff. Leave it lie.'

'They said the round and the punch. I went in and it didn't even go three rounds. I danced with him for two. Then I give him that one good one. Slap. And there he is on the canvas, sleeping for a week. That crowd was yelling for me good. I'll never have a night like that again. But that wasn't the end of it. Those boys was out several bundles and they had to put me down. Those boys was all over me that night on the way to the party on the boat.'

He rubbed the scar on his nose with a light finger, as if he could feel the chain opening it up again, and the boot that broke his skull and concussed him for twenty-three days.

'Then,' he said, 'you come in swinging and save me from breathing water. That caused you a lot of trouble. That I don't forget.'

We both stared at nothing for a while before Cliff's shaky voice trembled into the room again.

'They done me good. No more gloves for this boy when them doctors fix me up to walk. A tiny crack in my head you need a special machine to see. That stop me where I hurt. A tiny crack.'

I got up out of the chair and touched his shoulder; said: 'Come on, Cliff. Show me where the motor is. Talking that all through again won't get you a pension.'

He turned his head and looked sad.

'You don't get it, boy. Nothing I said. I owe you for living this life. That's what I'm saying. But you owe the other people. They can only lose if you start something with that set of faces.'

'I heard you, Cliff. Like you was on the right end of a megaphone. But you don't get the half of it. They ran Ronny down today. Broke him up inside with a taxi. All he did was pass me the money they owed. And they hurt him for that. For nothing.'

'They did that?' he said. He sounded like he was talking from the bottom of a treacle tin.

'The car, Cliff,' I said.

He nodded then, just once, sharply as though he was brushing a cobweb from his face.

'I'll get it out,' he said.

I could hear the old joanna being banged from the end of the street, rolling through *Marta*. A funny, lonely sound in the early evening. It was a quarter to seven and still light, but overcast and humid.

A tram hummed along the High Street three turnings away, and a dog barked from an area the other side of the street. Mums and dads sat around on their front steps in their turbans and chokers, fags on and pipes going. One old girl had her chair out on the pavement. A mixed bunch of kids played hopscotch, the grid and numbers chalked down the middle of the street. A boy and his girl lolled under a lamp-post sharing whispers. I reckoned he was in his own street and she was a visitor. If it was the other way round, he was chancing his arm.

I leaned up against the brass rail round the window of the pub and peered through the carved and frosted glass into the public bar. There were two old biddies sitting in the window seat cuddling a couple of flat glasses of stout, three old jossers up at the bar talking ferrets and whippets, and Ernie in the corner with his nose down in a pint and the racing page of the *Star*. The front page had some gubbins about proposed black-out drill and the word *Germany* in heavy italic, and a sub-head I couldn't read. The clock over the bar was six minutes fast.

I pushed the door and went in. One of the old jossers moved his arm so that I could get up to the bar to order. I got two lights by the neck, glasses upturned over them. I palmed the barman the right coins and sat down beside Ernie, shoving one of the bottles at him. He poured it without looking at me.

'All right,' I said, 'you're mysterious enough. Just for Chrissake don't talk out of the corner of your mouth.'

He gave me a sad look. The piano from the saloon bar tinkled about in high register, then began to vamp through *Three Jews from Jerusalem.*

I said: 'Who's been in? Anybody?'

Ernie thought for what seemed like a long time, then said: 'Like who we know. That what you mean?'

'Yeah,' I said. There didn't seem to be anything else to say.

'Only old Painful. Came in for the one before the first post at Harringay.'

That was what I wanted to hear.

'He'll likely be back before the day's older. He likes to keep his whistle wet.'

'Talk of the devil,' said Ernie through the left half of his mouth. The door creaked inward and an old bent man shuffled over to the bar. The other old jossers kept their eyes on their beer and wouldn't look at him. Mumping drinks didn't make anybody popular, and Painful had done a lot of it in his time.

He was a mass of crooks and bends, his head thrust out on the end of his neck, hands deep in the pockets of his worn jacket. His eyes were deep-sunk, blue with yellow whites. His nose jutted, a riot of strawberry veins and liver-spots, a dewdrop quivering below his nostrils. He moved his arm to wipe it away.

I'd never known him look any other way, but my old man had. When he'd worked out on the racecourses touting, Painful had been a useful bantam, taking on all comers in the boxing booths for a fiver a go. He'd only taken the count once, when a rival shower put a pro in against him, two stone heavier and as fast as a river. Painful wouldn't go down until his jaw was broken. Too much pride.

When he'd come round, the booth and his manager were long gone, and he was left to heal on his own.

He went with one of the old bookies as a bodyguard then, jacking the fight game in for good. One afternoon he stood up to three chancers that jumped his governor in the car park at Kempton. They got nothing, but Painful took a shiv in the gut and another crack in his jaw. He was three months in hospital getting over that.

I nudged Ernie. 'Buy him a drink.'

Ernie looked at me.

'That's right,' I said. 'Bust that two bob bit and get him one in. His tongue's hanging out like mine.'

Ernie elbowed his way to the bar. I waved Painful over and sat him down. He looked furtive.

'Bung me the slip, son. If you want a bet.'

'Not me, let the doggies run. Just thought you'd like a wet.'

Painful smiled, showing his gums.

'Won't say no.'

'Any time. Have a smoke.'

He held up his hand and waved it.

'Don't use them, do I, son? Me tubes, you know. Copped a lungful of mustard at Wipers. One puff and I'd cough up me ring.'

'So you would. I should have remembered.'

'No harm done. Pray God you never see nothing like it. I was one of the lucky baskets that come home, where there's a lot didn't.'

Ernie came back with the drinks.

' 'Ere you are then, gaffer,' he said, handing Painful a bottle and a glass. We all said 'Cheers', poured and drank.

'Hymie keep you busy?' I asked.

Painful wiped his mouth with the back of his hand and nodded.

'Mister Hyman?' he said. 'He keeps me on the go all right. But I don't begrudge. I don't have to take no charity from those toffee-noses down the Wesleyan or the Sally. I still got me respect.'

'Dead right,' I said. 'He must trust you a lot, carrying all them slips about. In and out of the office with all that money about the place.'

Painful wiped his mouth again.

'Dead finicky is Mister Hyman. He won't move without one of Spanner's boys with him. On a big night he has Spanner down there hisself with a couple of the boys. Shooters and everything.'

I laughed in his face and said:

'Where's the sense? Who's gonna try anything with Spanner's firm. Nobody.'

'I said that to Laurie one time. I said, Mister Laurie, who'd come waltzing in here and have a go with big faces like you about the place? It would take a bloke with four sides to his head to think he could get away with it. It wouldn't be, you know, sensible. You know what he said?'

'No, what did Laurie say?' I said, like it was easy.

'He laughed right out. Straight. He laughed and said that if people was sensible there wouldn't be no money there in the first place.'

Painful shook his head.

'There's times when I don't understand that Laurie. He's a lot better than most of the bleeders who hang about up there, but he do have a funny way of talking.'

'So I've heard,' I said. Ernie shot me a look but nothing showed in my face to give him any help. He dipped his finger in his beer and dabbed at the table top. The governor leaned over the bar.

'My slip go in, Painful? I just had Benny Fish on the blower from Harringay and me first one's up.'

'Don't you worry none, guv. Mister Hyman took care of yours personal. Always does.'

'Balls,' said the governor, ducking back out of sight.

'That Laurie sounds a fair feller,' I said. 'Keep the others off your neck, does he? Stop them pushing you around?'

'He does too. Don't see much of him nowadays, him being Mister Spandrell's right hand. It's that Poncer that's such a bastard. Nasty with it and all. He had me down the stairs the other day. Put his foot out and had me arse over tip. Laurie gave him a right rucking. I thought he was going to do him. Still, that Poncer's been moved over to the club now, and we got a new bloke starting tonight.'

'That's handy,' I said. 'You know him?'

'No. Except his name's Jacko and he's been about a bit.'

'Hadn't you better be getting back? We don't want to get you in bad with Hymie.'

Painful looked down at his empty glass then up at the clock.

'Plenty of time for another,' he said. 'They don't bag up till after the last race. I just get there for the last knockings about half eleven I suppose. Be in bed by one. Course, Saturday's later. But you expect that with all the meetings up and down the country, not counting the dogs.'

'Another time,' I said, standing up. 'See you around, Painful.'

He smiled down at the coins I dropped on the table, nodding and rubbing the end of his nose.

'Teddah, boys.'

We stepped out onto the pavement into the heavy dusk. Clouds heaved overhead, full of rain. Most of the people had gone indoors to do what people did on a Saturday night. The boy and his girl were still under the lamp with their heads closer, sharing a cigarette. The hopscotch game was deserted.

'Where's the car?' said Ernie. 'You got it all right?'

'Mostly I've got an appetite,' I said. 'Come on.'

We walked east.

I recrossed my arms and leaned against the side window of the jeweller's shop, careful to stay in the shadows. Kids had broken the glass and mantle of the gas lamp across the street so that only the pilot light flickered. It barely showed the lamp housing let alone the pavement. Light spilled from a chink in the window blind over Hymie's window, now and again somebody moved behind it, throwing shadows. Somewhere a clock bonged twelve times.

Ten minutes later the door across the street opened with a faint tinkle. Painful emerged and shuffled off down the street, looking neither right nor left. I could hear him long after he had disappeared. I lit up a careful cigarette, smoking it cupped in my hand, down inside my upturned collar. Time sauntered by.

The light behind the blind went out. I dropped the cigarette, crossed the road in a run and flattened myself up against the brickwork by the door. A lock rattled and feet started down the stairs. I struck a match and jammed it into the box. The heads flared and I tossed the blazing mess into the gutter. The headlamps of a car blinked on down the street as it pulled out from the kerb and cruised forward.

The doorbell tinkled and a face under a snap-brimmed hat poked out to stare at the burning matchbox. I stepped out and grabbed his lapels, setting myself and pulling him around in a circle. His feet came up off the ground as I swung him into the wall. His face slapped against the bricks. When I let him go he slid onto the pavement with his feet wide and his eyes closed.

Hymie looked down at him with his satchel hanging off the end of his arm. It took him all his time and effort to look at me.

'Jesus Christ,' he said.

I held out my hand and he passed the satchel. It was heavy, which was as it should be. The car eased into the kerb with the back door yawning.

'Tell Spandrell, when you see him,' I said, 'his protection needs protecting.'

'I know you,' said Hymie.

'I know you do,' I said, and slid sideways into the car.

Hymie watched us drive away without moving. I leaned out and closed the door as Ernie took the corner on two wheels. It started to rain.

Five

The rain came down in rods, snapping and sputtering on the road and rolling in black tides down the gratings. It drummed on the bonnet of the car, making steam. The metal ticked as it cooled. The other side of the street was almost obscured by the spray. Ernie smoked without using his hands, as I watched the Square Ring Club.

The marquee lights were still on over the entrance, a couple of hundred bulbs lighting up half the street. A yellow soft-edged glow in the wetness. I knew what the inside looked like without having to go in.

It was a long room with tables each side of a centre reservation and curtained alcoves along the walls, a table inside each with a chair on either side. You can imagine who used those when a girl was there for the asking but there might be a chance the wife could walk in. At the far end was a bandstand and a pocket-sized square of parquet flooring for six determined people to dance on.

In the middle of all the tables was a raised dais with ropes around like a boxing ring. The table in the centre of the ring could seat a round dozen. That's where Spanner entertained his particular friends and people he wanted to impress. Some surprising people ended up sitting on those chairs.

The whole place was decorated in purple and gold. The drapes, tablecloths, carpet and upholstery in purple, chairs, woodwork and the menus in gold. Not to my taste.

Headlights washed across the KEEP THIS ENTRANCE

CLEAR signs either side of the parking-lot gates and a black Daimler bounced into the road. Ernie came upright in his seat, an inch of ash falling from his cigarette.

'That the one?' he said.

'Yeah.'

We were in third gear before the Daimler turned the corner. We followed it back to Hymie's, pulling in three car-lengths behind it. Hymie was standing in the rain, the shoulders of his camel-hair coat were black. He leaned forward to wave his arms about at somebody sitting in the back seat. Cigar smoke rolled out at him. The bloke I'd slammed into the wall was leaning in the doorway on rubbery legs. He looked like he wanted to apologise to somebody if they'd let him. His hat was still on the pavement getting rained on.

'Don't look well, do he?' said Ernie.

The Daimler pulled away in a shower of spray with Hymie still talking. He didn't have time to dodge back and save his trousers. As we drove past him I gave him a wave. His mouth opened wider than I'd have thought possible. The snap-brimmed hat skidded across the pavement as our spray hit it.

The Daimler swept through the mean streets, taking corners with a lot of tailswing, not wasting time. It finally turned into a terraced row with sleek tiled roofs and dark windows.

'This is where your old dosser was, Bergie,' said Ernie. 'They've definitely tumbled.' He pulled in at the corner with the motor running. 'What now?' The brim of his cap shook with tension. I picked the black satchel off the back seat and opened the door.

'I'm getting out. Get the jam-jar stowed and I'll see you at Dotty's for breakfast. Right?'

Ernie opened and closed his mouth several times.

'Go home, Ernie. Sling it.'

He drove away slowly, splashing through the puddles. I got under the railway bridge and watched the Daimler. It was a long time before anybody got out. Somebody wiped the inside of the back window and peered out. I could see other faces at the sides. A match flared as they all lit up. I counted four cigarettes apart from the cigar. I was too far away to see individual faces.

Three men, then a fourth left the car and went quickly up the path to number fourteen. There was a flash of light on a wire as they came up against the front door, then the path was empty.

I walked out from under the bridge, opened the offside back door of the Daimler and got in. Spandrell looked at me as I dropped the satchel in his lap.

'Close the door,' he said, 'you'll get rain on the upholstery.'

I closed the door. I watched him pulling on his cigar and he watched me watching him. The car was filled with the smell of leather, wet clothes and smoke. A warm cocoon in the rain. I wanted to light up myself but I thought I might need my hands free.

'You're a bit of a cucumber, ain't you?' said Spandrell. 'You kick the slats out of one of my collectors and then bring back the poppy before you've had time to count it. What do you think that buys you?'

'A job,' I said.

'Whose job?'

'The bloke who fell against the wall won't be needing his,' I said. 'That'll do for a start.'

'For a start, eh?'

Spandrell flicked ash into the tray set in the back of the driver's seat, carefully, to save the carpet. Then he put the cigar back into his mouth, rolling it to one side between his teeth.

'For a start,' I said. He nodded at that.

'The thing about starts,' he said, 'is they're sort of temporary. You know what I mean. For a start it's Jacko. You spread his nose all over his face for a start. Then after a bit it seems like there's somewhere else you'd like to be. A bit higher, with a bit more pay in it. Then maybe just to simplify things you do some more nose-spreading. That what you had in mind, boy?'

'No,' I said.

'You say. I'll say this for you, boy. You've got more front than Woolworth's, and they're in every high street.'

I grinned at him, trying not to sweat. His eyes hadn't moved off my face.

'You look like trouble to me, Bergman. I've got some good boys working for me, do anything, they will. But there's one thing about them I can count on. The one thing I like.'

He tapped his forehead.

'They don't think for themselves too much. Not that they couldn't, but they don't. You're a born independent. Believe me, that's a compliment. But you wouldn't sit right in a firm like mine. You couldn't keep your mind from working. Trying to change the odds, watching your chances. You see what I mean?'

'No,' I lied.

He sighed, took his cigar from his mouth, looked at the ash, and put it back into his mouth. It seemed to roll to the corner on its own.

'You think I don't know about you and Laurie?' he asked.

'What about me and Laurie?'

'You've got a grudge. Right or wrong, one way or the other don't make my tummy rumble, you got a grudge about Laurie. He says you reckon you did time because of him. Two-stretch. It's been spoke about by more than one out of the Ville. Bergman's got a down on Laurie, tell him take cover. It's all over.'

'Do I look like I'm sweating?' I said.

He was about to answer when the doors opened and somebody caught me round the neck, pulling my right arm up behind me. I pushed out my left arm to grab the back of the seat, caught it and started to heave myself upright when something banged down into the back of my hand. I couldn't move it. A wooden handle and an inch of blade showed above it. There was a big initial L carved in it.

A fist caught me in the side of the face, punching me back into the seat, then another, higher on the temple. I saw faces, close and hot before the pain carried me into darkness filled with exploding grey balloons. Then it was just dark.

'He's coming out of it,' somebody said.

'That's easily handled,' said somebody else.

'Hold off,' said Spandrell. 'I'll say when.'

Things came back quickly. I was upright, I knew. Somebody, two people, were holding me up by my arms. I couldn't move my feet because something cut into them, holding them together. My left arm and hand pulsed hot and swollen. I opened my eyes enough to see.

Spandrell stood between two men, one of them was dark and grinning, the other was Laurie. He wasn't smiling like I remembered he did. His face was white and stretched, like canvas on bone, bleached under his yellow hair. He wore a grey pinstripe with a white handkerchief in the breast pocket. His trousers entirely covered his shoes.

Spandrell got hold of my hair and pulled my head up.

'Can you hear me, Bergman?' he said.

I looked at him.

'This ain't gonna be quick for you. You're a God-send, believe me. An example. We're gonna hang you out. The tide can have you, but not the fishes. We want you found so the word'll go round. Nobody touches Spanner's patch. Got it?'

He twisted his fingers in my hair.

'Got it,' I said.

A tug hooted down the river and oily water lapped up through the boards we were standing on. It was dark and the rain had given way to a light drizzle. I smelled the hot night air through my swollen nostrils, catching a whiff of the puke on my clothes. There were lights on the far bank, bobbing on wires above the silhouetted gantries. Spandrell let go of my hair.

'He's yours, Laurie, Poncer.'

I heard him walk away before the first punch hit me low down. There was a second and a third, but I was going away fast to fall down the pit with no sides, no colour, no bottom. I fell for a long time.

Six

There wasn't any pain. It was around me though, stalking me; prowling. I thought about moving, there was an up and a down and I was floating in a soft-hardness that could have been water or mud. Somehow it didn't matter, I just had to get up. I tried for it, swimming without using my arms or my legs. I couldn't anyway, they were tied to weights. Breathing was hard, somebody had put iron globes where my lungs used to be. Why would they do that? They hit me, though. I remembered that. Shoved a knife through my hand. A knife with Laurie's initial carved in the handle. I was there when he carved it. A rainy afternoon with nothing on at the pictures. Wetness I remembered too. The knife must have ruined the Daimler's leather upholstery.

The wetness rode up in my throat like a flood of paste spilling out of my nostrils, warm and tasting of rivers. Air swept into the iron globes, swelling them like old leather, creaking like bellows. A sound like Poncer's laugh. I went after his face and found it grinning with too many teeth through the punches. He grunted and laughed and punched. Better. The leather was supple and moving the air about on its own. Find Laurie now.

Smiling now, like he used to when we had an office above the greengrocer's. An old room, really, where he schemed schemes and was lavish with enthusiasm. But a friend was expendable when a profit was to be split. I moved my arm but a tube held it, and tape and sheets; crisp with a hospital smell. I opened my eyes and reminded myself how to use them.

There was a horizon with a grid across it, silver metal with the top corners rounded. I counted the bars but they repeated into infinity. I let the lids roll down all the way.

Something held my right wrist with cool-warm fingers and there was a light ticking. I had to use my eyes and turn my head as I focussed. A nurse was taking my pulse. She saw my eyes open and she gave me a hard professional smile.

'Hello,' she said, 'would you like a drink?'

Somehow she knew I did without me having to say anything. She dropped my wrist and clacked away across the hard floor. Liquid gurgled from a bottle and a tap ran, then she was back with her arm circling my neck and a cold glass against my mouth.

'Rinse your mouth and spit.'

I gulped some cherry-flavoured stuff and she wiped my chin. I couldn't spit. She supported my head with one hand and plumped my pillow. I had to ask her where I was but it came out as 'Wassis play.'

She dropped my head back on the pillow and brushed my lips with her fingers. They felt nice.

'Please don't try to talk. You're in hospital. We'll take care of you.'

She patted my shoulder and clicked away. The room went away then and I was in darkness again, but warm and resting. It was like that for a long time. Then there was buzzing and a chair scraping and a woman shushed whoever moved the chair.

I looked straight at a copper with his helmet in his lap. He pulled a *London Opinion* from his pocket and started to read, moving his lips. I went back into the darkness with a feeling of sadness rolling with me.

I was running again, on the spot, with glue in my shoes and black hounds panting after me. I ran with my mouth open, trying to make a sound in the rushing silence. I was going down in the flaming water, it was running down my throat and I was choking with nobody listening but the hounds as they bit at my back and my thighs and my feet. I couldn't run. The burning was over me now, inside and out, burning like ice. I tried to turn and hit out at the looming things with no faces and ripping teeth. They hacked and clawed and I was in pieces over the landscape. They trampled and fought each other over and inside me, on and on and on...

The voices overhead and nothing to do with me. Not listening.

'Nurse. You'd better come. He's bleeding from the mouth.'

'It's a haemorrhage. Who's on duty in Surgical?'

'Mister Gibson, Sister.'

'Get him to come up right away.'

'Yes, Sister.'

'And get that stupid policeman out of the way.'

'In here, Mister Gibson.'

'Down to the operating room straight away. We'll prepare him on the way. No, I can't wait for porters.'

'Hold that drip up, girl.'

Nothing.

A trolleybus had one of its front tyres over my face, pushing my head through the tarblocks and the gravel and the stones the Romans had used to build their first roads. Underneath there had to be flaking bones and fossils of things that had hopped and slithered before men had stood upright and reached for a rock to hit something with. I couldn't take any more pushing without not being there any more. I tensed my face muscles, clenched my jaw, set my teeth and forced my eyelids apart.

I was looking at a ceiling, white glossed and gleaming with sunlight. The door through the end of the bed had an observation port in its upper part. Through the glass was a circle of corridor wall with a light switch on it. A nurse's head blurred past.

Without looking I knew the copper was sitting in his chair. I heard his magazine rustle. I turned my head away and there he was, looking right back at me.

'Well,' he said, 'it's about time you came back to the land of the living. Been out for days.'

Even his whisper could have stopped the mighty roar of London's traffic. Violets, lovely violets. Bear down son, you're light-headed.

'Been right busy in here while you been bye-byes. Missed it all, didn't you? Had the surgeon up for close on all night two nights running. Poor bloke needs a holiday after all that.'

His voice went through me like fingernails on glass. I would have hit him in his great pudding face if I hadn't been made of hurting putty. My whole face was swollen and the edges of my nostrils seemed to be tickling my ear lobes. At least my fingers wiggled when I told them to.

'Want a drink or something?' asked the copper. 'I'll call the nurse. I've got to get on the blower anyway, seeing you're awake.'

He went out without waiting for me to answer. The nurse came in before the door had a chance to close fully. We went through the temperature-taking and the blood-pressure-measuring. Another nurse brought me some soup in an invalid cup and fed me, both of them mouthing the comforting things that seem to go with the uniform.

The man in the white coat came in and hummed over his clip-board and had the nurses pull back the sheets so that he could sound my chest and look at his handiwork under the pads and bandages. He probed my ribs with his cold fingers and I thought I had been shot. He looked sympathetic but it didn't make the pain go away. My eyes leaked and both the nurses rushed to wipe off my chin. Bloody humiliating.

They tucked me up again and left me looking at the

shining ceiling. I could hear the buzz of visitors making relatives' chat along the corridors. A fly buzzed too, banging against the window until he found the way out. Then he was gone and it was just me throbbing under the bedclothes and the ceiling reflecting the sunlight. I was asleep before I knew it.

It was dark when I came to. The light was on and the copper had a different face and he was reading a newspaper. When he saw that I was awake he got up and went out without a word. When he came back he had another man with him. Somebody I knew, but didn't want to.

He was heavy and middle-aged, with a florid fleshy face and at least three chins. Grey flashed in his sideboards, the rest of his hair was jet. His eyes were almost luminous, with black pupils. He wore a dark blue herringbone under his police raincoat with an early rose in his buttonhole. He carried a black homburg and a rolled copy of *The Times*. A snappy dresser was Inspector Lemmon.

He stood at the end of the bed for a while before making himself comfortable in the copper's chair.

'Shall I stay, sir?' asked the constable. He had a boy's voice.

'Wait in the car,' said Lemmon. That's all he did say until the constable was well down the passage. Then:

'Well, Bergman.'

'Well, Mister Lemmon.'

'Didn't take you long to get in deep, did it? And that's not a pun.'

'Not long.'

'No.'

He took a packet of Players out of his pocket, played with it for a bit, then put it away.

'Three cracked ribs, one broken. A deep cut through the left hand, missing the tendons, luckily, lacerations, facial contusions and an internal haemorrhage. That'll cut your tennis down a bit, I should think.'

'Wimbledon can do without me. So can you. Why don't you stop wasting my time? And yours.'

'I should have thought you'd wasted more time than me, Bergman. Twenty-four months of porage. Now who knows how long in this place.'

'It's a rest cure. Somewhere for me to receive my friends.'

He enjoyed saying the next thing. Almost licking his lips.

'There are some friends I'd think would be anxious to come calling. Nice open hospital with the pigeon trussed ready for the oven. Probably the first time the host was eaten by the guests.'

He laughed then, one hard bark. I made a face.

'Ho, fucking ho,' I said.

'Why don't you cough, son? You're tying up too much of the Met's manpower, having big strong coppers sitting around holding your bedpan for you. You should see my crime figures, discouraging.'

'You should see mine,' I said.

'Zero to date, according to you.'

It would have been handy to have made an expressive gesture but I only had my mouth and eyes to work with. I waggled my eyebrows. And that was tiring. I said:

'You'd have me back inside whatever I said. So why say anything? No percentage.'

'Without your plates touching,' he said with another little bark.

I left my eyebrows where they were.

'You were caught red-handed on that Moorgate pussy job. Right there in the yard with the stuff heaped in the lorry, your mates standing around with their mouths open. You'd have done seven with them if they hadn't said you weren't there. Still say it, I'm told.'

'Nice of them,' I said.

'I thought so. Honour amongst thieves and all that sort of thing.'

'You read the wrong sort of books.'

'It's you that tends to deal in fiction, Bergman. Me, I work with facts. They make up into long boring reports, pages of the stuff.'

He said a lot more of that kind of thing. I felt myself drifting off away from him. I could see that yard outside the fur store, the lorry and Ernie with an arm full of the stuff. He had seen me as I dropped off the wall onto the cobbles.

'Bergie.' His voice had sounded full of sweat.

I grabbed him and slammed him up against the side of the lorry.

'I told you no.'

'But it's a guaranteed four hundred notes, Bergie, mate. I couldn't turn it down. Let up, we're nearly through.'

I hit him then. Twice across the face.

'You've probably rung alarms in every nick between here and Maidstone. I told you it wasn't on without a good wire man. I told you stay off it.'

'Let up, Bergie. We're nearly through.'

The yobs on the job with him had made a circle around us. One of them caught at me round the neck.

'Come on out of it, Bergman. You didn't want any. Piss off.'

I pushed my elbow back into his middle and he flailed off into a huddle on the ground. The others watching on tiptoe.

'You burkes!' I said. 'You've been conned. It's a bloody set-up. There won't be a fence in this town who'll touch this stuff. You were wanted out of the way. You make too many waves, all of you. Amateurs, a bunch of three-rounders.'

'Do him,' said one. 'It's him that's conning. Johnny in the Garden gave me his hand on it.'

They came in at me then in a rush, grunting and thrashing, too many to do any good. Then the bells rang and the law car banged open the gates and had us in its headlights. The boys panicked and ran in all directions. I grabbed Ernie under the crutch and heaved. He went over the wall and out of sight. I stepped back and made a jump for the top with my arms out. A truncheon caught me across the back, emptying my lungs. I went down as I was hit across the back of the neck. I stayed awake long enough to know I'd been conned too. Laurie's call had got me there just in time. He had set the job, and would walk away without a backward glance.

Lemmon's hand was on my shoulder. I shrugged him off and hurt myself. There was sweat on my top lip.

'I'm listening,' I said. I was wet from head to foot.

'I said, who's to know?'

'I'd know. That's who. If I bubbled. Meaning *if* I had something to bubble about. I'd know. I got like this because I was real careless. I fell in the docks. Must have had a bevy too many. Now you've got what you wanted. Have an early night. Take your old lady to the pictures. She'd be pleased to see you, I know.'

He went on as though I hadn't said anything. Maybe I hadn't. The way I felt I wouldn't have known either way.

'And you got yourself tied up to a stanchion just below high-water mark all by yourself. Clever that. The Harry Houdini of Hackney.'

'I do card tricks too.'

'Come off it, son. If one of the night-watchmen hadn't been busy with his torch you'd be there yet. As it was you'd swallowed enough to float the Mary on. You're dead lucky.'

'That's me,' I said. 'The king of Crown and Anchor.' I was running out of witty things to say.

'All right, Bergman, have it your way. There's more law round this place than at a saluting parade at Hendon.

Just waiting. You know what this is?'

He held up a headed card and an envelope.

'One of Morrie Hyman's betting slips. You write out your bet and either hand it to one of his runners, or post it through his door. With me so far?'

I looked at the end of the bed.

'I've written something on this one and I'm going to see it gets posted. It says: Bergman is in the Seamen's Mercy. If you want him. You see how my mind's working?'

I could see in six-foot capitals. He licked the envelope and smoothed the flap down.

'No postage stamp required, either. It's not going to cost me a thing.'

I worked up a smile around my nose.

'I'd like to see Hymie. A good mate of mine. Maybe he'll get some of the boys to drop by. Listen, you might just write the visiting times down so's they don't waste a trip.'

'You can bet they won't.'

He stood up putting on his hat.

'Teddah, Mister Lemmon.'

'Maybe it's goodbye,' he said quietly, then he was gone.

Seven

I pressed the buzzer for the nurse.

'What, again?' she said, coming in and throwing back the bedclothes.

'Must have a weak bladder.'

'It matches my head,' she smiled, 'the times I run in here to carry you around the place.'

I got my arm around her shoulders and swung my legs over the side of the bed, leaning more than was strictly necessary. We waltzed down the passage to the lavatory. She held the door open for me to slide through, then the door was shut and I was on my own with the Thomas Crapper.

I climbed up onto the bowl and eased the window open. A breeze came in off the river with overtones of oily brine. The tide was out and there were birds fluttering about on the mud flats.

'Don't lock the door, and call out when you want to go back. I'll hear you.'

'Thanks,' I said.

There was a deep sill below the window, Portland Stone cemented into the red brick. There was a lot of it all over the building; heavily carved and grimed. I was on the third and top floor where they kept the few private patients they got, mostly shipping people, with the odd nob from the City thrown in.

A canopy grew out over the front entrance. It had a flat roof and stone lions rampant at each corner. Beyond was a forecourt with a high boundary wall and a pair of wrought-iron gates permanently ajar. An ambulance stood in one of the marked parking bays. Buses rumbled on the other side of the wall.

Beyond the traffic was a grey row of terraced flats with all the decoration at roof level; the sort that Peabody built. He should have been forced to live in one when the rubbish chutes got blocked and the lavs packed up.

I got a grip on the sill and leaned out with one foot hooked behind the lavatory downpipe. The left edge of the building was three rooms and a wedge of carving away; a series of portraits of famous surgeons set in wreaths, running down to the leading edge of the canopy.

To the side was a small walled yard with two garages, one open, a row of waste bins and a ladder leaning against the wall. A man in shirtsleeves was cleaning a black Bentley and whistling in a dull monotone.

I eased down onto the pan, then onto the floor, closed the window and gave the chain a tug. The Crapper flushed like a frantic cataract. The nurse was waiting.

'All right?' she said.

'Handsome,' I said.

'Here we go then.'

The relief copper was standing by the chair when we got back. He had a pile of *Picture Posts* and *Everybody's*.

'He's been nicking in the waiting room again, nurse,' I said as she tucked me in.

'Now, Mister Bergman,' said the nurse, 'we had enough of that nonsense yesterday.'

'Well, I still say it was him that had the "Now wash your hands" away. He's got mean eyes.'

'Watch it,' said the copper. It was the one with the shout and the pudding face. We didn't like each other. That was my fault. He'd been decent enough, but that wasn't the way I wanted it.

'Go on, ask him where my toothpaste got to.'

'I will not,' she said. 'The idea. Any more and I'll have the matron in to you.'

'It wasn't her. She doesn't clean her teeth. Shaves, though.'

The copper's face was like a pink balloon. The nurse shushed me and went out. Pudding and I were alone.

'Siddown before you fall down,' I said. He was already half way down. He paused with his buttocks out.

'You mouthy bastard,' he said. 'I hope they do come and carve you. I'm buggered if I'm gonna stop them.'

I pumped my pillows up under my head and said: 'Who's asking?'

He picked up a magazine and went down into the chair.

'You know,' he said, 'if they do top you with no known relatives and all, you'll end up in a place like this anyway. For students to practise on. Pickle you first so you don't rot, and then take you apart layer by layer. Highly delicious. Shouldn't mind watching that myself.'

'I'll leave the best part to you in my will,' I said. 'Give you something to suck on when the inspector's gone home.'

'Watch your mouth, Bergman.'

'Please, keep your voice down. I need my afternoon nap. I'm not a well man.'

I turned my head away with my lids down to think about other things.

Pudding woke me up when he had a stretch and a yawn and his chair creaked. I made a production of having a yawn myself. The overhead lights were off in the room and the copper was reading by the spill from the bed-light. Every second light was off in the passage. The observation port was a grey circle. I took a squint at my watch. It was just gone eleven. The night staff had been on half an hour and Pudding was an hour away from being relieved. He had an *Everybody's* right up in front of his face so that he didn't have to look at me. That suited me fine.

I dropped my pillows to the floor one at a time. He didn't notice. I unhooked the metal pillow rest from the bedhead, sat up in bed all the way with it at the end of my arms, and brought it down on top of his head. For a bit nothing happened. Then, very slowly, with the magazine straight out before him, he rolled sideways onto the floor.

I could hardly breathe. My chest was tight and constricted from the effort. Liver spots danced all over the room. I lay back for a bit and let the pain go. It took its time.

I got the bedclothes off me and squatted beside the prone pudding. He was breathing through his nose. He had a lump under his hair but the skin wasn't split. It took me for ever to get him out of his uniform and into the bed. I left the pillows on the floor so that he wouldn't suffocate and got dressed in the jacket, trousers and boots. He wasn't that much bigger than me except in the seat. I left his helmet under the chair and let myself into the passage.

There was a light coming from under the matron's door, and her voice; low, as she talked into a telephone. Evidently Mister Saxby was responding to treatment. His bowels had made a lovely motion that morning.

I went into the lavatory and shot the bolt. The window was open and the night smelled of burnt cork. I sat on the bowl and got the boots untied, looped the laces together and slung them around my neck. I tried thinking of all the things to stop me going out through the window. There wasn't one.

The Portland sill was gritty through Pudding's socks when I slid down onto it with my face against the bricks. I inched sideways watching the windowsills go past above me. One, then another, and much later the last before the portraits. I put out my foot and waved it in mid-air. Nothing. I pulled back and had a look down.

The sill ended a good yard before the frieze started. I stood there having a sweaty think.

A bus went past behind and below me and a car squealed on a corner. The breeze played with my hair.

There was a soilpipe running down the wall above me at a shallow angle. I stretched up and reached it easily with my left hand. I'd have to take my whole weight on that hand as I swung across the gap and caught the top of the first wreath. I didn't know if it would hold me with that bloody great gash in it.

I reached up, gripped, and swung. A million volts hit me in the knuckles. I scrabbled with a wild right arm as I lost my grip on the pipe. I was going down with air between all my fingers, thinking of all the people I'd wake up when I landed. Pudding laughing and selling me for surgical soup, Laurie smiling like he always did as he read about it in the papers, Spandrell laughing his socks down and letting everyone think it was down to him, Ernie dropping dirt onto the coffin and once in a while forgetting to buy flowers, Dotty and Lemmon shrugging and indifferent.

Then I was just hanging there.

Hanging there looking up Joseph Lister's nose. Something had given under the bandages and a film of warmth was running down my side. I hooked my toes over the carved laurel leaves and had a rest. Lister's chin was cool against my face.

I stepped down onto the next head, got a toehold in his moustache, a grip on his eyebrows, and was face to face with one of the Hunter brothers. I climbed down three more faces without much trouble. Then I stepped onto Hippocrates' bald head. He was obviously the pigeons' favourite. The next thing I knew I was flat on my back on the canopy looking up at the stars.

I rolled the elephant off my chest and got onto my hands and knees, shuffling across the leads and dropping down onto the wall around the yard. Somehow I pulled the ladder to where I needed it and somehow I climbed onto the top rungs and hung there with the uniform holding me up. Every direction seemed to be down.

Somebody said something.

I listened so hard my head hurt.

'Come on down,' the somebody said.

I had to, anyway, before my legs gave way. I think a glacier could have beat me to the bottom. I was turned round and pushed back against the ladder, patted for concealed anything, then just looked at.

'Hello, Laurie,' I said. 'I thought you'd come if it was anyone.'

'It's me,' he said. Light ran down the blade in his hand. I nodded. He'd changed his suit to a black one with a thin chalk-stripe. Only his chin showed from the shadow of his hat. There was nothing behind him but the far wall. The garages were closed and the man that whistled over the Bentley was nowhere to be seen. Even the waste bins had their lids hard down.

'If you hadn't been so clever you'd be in a nice snug cell now, Bergie. But you had to try it your way.'

He was right. I nodded some more to let him know. Let him talk. Let him use up the night. I wasn't going anywhere.

'One thing,' I said. 'Why Ronny? Did you have to chop him that way? That won't help you with your old friends.'

'They're U/S, old son. All for the chop. There's no room for them.'

'Everybody goes, eh? When's Spanner's turn?'

His head went back enough to show me his smile. He was using all his teeth.

'Ah, Bergie. There's time enough.'

There was somebody behind Laurie now. Small and quick, with his arm crooked over his head. A short black tube in his fist.

'There's never enough time, old son. Take some advice. Do it quick, or don't do it.'

There was a low whistle as the cosh swung. Laurie's hat lost its shape, spinning off into the bins. He looked surprised, falling forward with his hair in his eyes. His knees hit the ground and his face slapped the gravel. Ernie hit him again on the back of the neck, a short swing from the shoulder.

'That'll hold the bastard,' he said.

'Finish him,' I said. 'Don't let him get up.'

Ernie got under my arm and got me stumbling away.

'Not even for you, Bergie mate. I ain't no topper.' He grunted, half carrying me. 'There's others who'll do for him.'

He got me out through the gate and down the back of the main block to where the forecourt started. He left me propped against the wall and went off round the corner. A starter whirred and coughed and the back of an ambulance backed towards me, the doors open, Ernie waving me on from the driver's seat.

I got up inside and flopped onto one of the stretchers. I heard the doors shut behind me. I noticed that the blankets were red before I passed out.

I was pushed and shoved and bumped down some steps. There was a knock, a bolt rattled and light flared. I screwed up my eyes as I was bundled inside and flopped into an armchair.

'He looks dead already,' said a hard woman's voice.

'This'll fix him. He's all right, I tell you.'

A bottle chinked on a glass and something burned in my mouth. I coughed to show I was still kicking and grabbed at the glass, tilting it all the way.

'Another one,' I managed. The bottle gurgled and I got the glass back. I emptied it in two.

I was in a basement room. The hard chairs and the sofa had a temporary look about them, as if they expected to be moved hurriedly. They'd looked that way ever since I was a kid, learning to take cigarette smoke all the way down and to spit straight. It was Manny's parlour. Manny the fixer, Manny the fence, Manny the money-lender. Manny with his back room where the dice rattled for as long as the money lasted.

He sat across from me in his old bentwood rocker under a litho portrait of Queen Mary wearing all her diamonds, a face growing out of sparkle. His eyes were just pouched slits in his stubbly face. He was smiling as sadly as ever, his arms crossed in front of his fairisle pull-over, his feet in carpet slippers. He was old and smelly and obliging.

When we were kids we used to think he was a Russian king with magical powers and we used to cross ourselves when we passed his door. Everybody knew there were thousands of bodies under the floorboards, poisoned by the sweets he used to give us all. We never ate them. We used to take one for later and drop it down the nearest drain, because if you didn't you'd die in agony and never be seen again except as a pile of bones in the dog-meat shop.

Dotty sat to his left, Cliff next to her and Ernie was standing over me with the Booth's London Dry in his hand.

'Whose birthday is it?' I said. Only Manny smiled.

'Look at the state of him,' said Dotty. 'I've seen better sights in a dog's bowl.'

'Lay off, Dot. Can't you see he's knackered?' said Ernie.

'He's that, all right,' she snorted, loud enough to shame a horse. 'And it's his own doing. You heard what Ernie said. Bloody clown.'

'You think I've dragged you into something, Dotty?' I said.

'All of us.'

'Much as I hate to correct a lady, you're dead wrong. If

I'd taken a tumble on the snide, you'd still be for the chop. I got it straight from the horse's mouth.'

I held the glass for Ernie to wet the bottom. They all watched as I put it away. Cliff rolled a slow cigarette using all his fingers, licked it along, put it in his mouth and spoke round it.

'All except me,' he whispered.

'That's the size of it. It'd be clever if you weren't here. Take off back to the garage. There's no percentage for Laurie in putting one on you. Go on, teddah,' said Ernie.

'Shut up,' said Manny.

We all looked at him. His expression was sadder if anything.

'Talk, talk,' he said. 'What's to talk? Did I ask you here? No. Did Bergie want you to come? No. Who's asking anything? Nobody. So what's to talk? I'll tell you. It ain't no big secret, neither. Spandrell's building for something. He wants everything. You were warned, but who listened, eh? Who wanted to know when I told you we needed to pool everything, just laughing in the face, that's what I got. Bergie was the only one who said "Yes, Manny" to old Manny. "You're right Manny." The only one. What happens?'

He spread his hands and looked at them one by one.

'I'll tell you. He's the first to be done down. Into the den with him. And this Laurie, he could see a good thing. Smart boy. He does for Bergman to show faith with the money man. Look, he says, I put down my friend. How's that for trustworthy? Come in, says the man. And you? Wailing now it gets uncomfortable for you. You turn on your own with blame. It's Bergie's fault. He's the one. A goat for the pharisees. Lead him out to them. Let us wash our hands and maybe Caesar will leave us alone. Stupid. Like children.'

He slumped back and for a brief moment a little white showed in his eyes.

'Go home,' he said to the ceiling.

Cliff unwound from his chair. He said:

'You know where I am, Bergie. For anything.'

'I know, Cliff.'

He went out on silent feet and the door snicked shut.

Manny's eyes stayed on the ceiling. Somehow he was staring at Dotty. Her bangles rattled as she emptied her glass. She banged it down and thumbed at Ernie.

'We know where the door is, Manny,' she said. 'From here on in I stay behind my own front door. There are too many complications the way you two play the game. This'll blow over. If only you had the sense to see it.'

'Bergie?' said Ernie. I shook my head at him.

'She's wrong, Ernie,' I said, 'but stay with her. She's gonna need somebody. It looks like you're elected. Stay close and be lucky.'

'Wish it for yourself,' sneered Dotty. 'It's you that needs all he can get.'

'Goodnight, Dotty. Thanks for the good wishes.'

She rattled stones in her throat and slammed the door behind them.

'Well, Manny,' I said.

He uncrossed his arms and leaned down behind his chair for a glass of stout. He took his time taking the top four inches in.

'That Dotty,' he said. 'Such a strong woman, but stupid.'

I yawned.

'For you, Bergie, I have made some arrangements. There's a car coming. You get into it and you don't talk to who's driving. You get taken to a place with doctors and fresh air. You stay until everything is better. When it's right to come back I'll send the car. Okay?'

'If that's the way you want it, Manny.'

'That's how.'

And that's how it was.

Eight

The thunder was over and around, racketing overhead in the rolling blackness of the rainclouds, splintered by the lightning that forked down onto the city. The roof was a dancing mass of rain-dollies around me, their heads whipping in the wind. The storm had been going on half the night, making up for the blackout with savage bursts of brilliance. Thunder clapped directly overhead and a sheet of lightning burned every detail into white relief. Every brick and line of mortar, each chimney pot and its stipple of grime. A huddled pigeon had wedged itself between the pots, its head under a wing, skin showing pink through its sodden feathers.

'You and me both,' I said. It didn't hear me.

I paddled across to the parapet, looking down to where the street should have been. Another flash showed it to me, a wet grey strip with unlit lamps, no traffic and the gutters awash; the marquee front of the Square Ring a black oblong studded with dead bulbs.

There was only one car in the club's parking lot, a soft-top Alvis.

The skylight opened with one heave and I stepped down into the loft above the club office. A chink of light coming up between the joists and the wall showed the loft was empty of clutter, just a layer of dust and the chain that lowered a ladder to the top landing. A typewriter ticked in bursts from below. I leaned on the chain to see that the lights were off and nobody was looking back. I used the chain some more and the foot of the ladder kissed the carpet without a sound. I went down.

The manager looked up from his two-finger typing as I stepped inside the office. His mouth smiled, the rest of him didn't. A cigarette curled smoke into his eyes from the centre of the smile. He blinked, looking like he wanted to wave it away, but his hands stayed on the keys with the fingers spread.

'We're closed,' he said. The cigarette bobbed ash into his lap.

'Up,' I said.

He stayed where he was until I took the gun out of my pocket. It wasn't that he moved fast, he just wasn't sitting down any more. I waved him around the desk. He had to push a drawer closed before he could get past the filing cabinets.

'Down,' I said.

He went down onto his knees in a slow sink with his eyes on my stomach. When he thought he was close enough he dived. He came straight in on my knee as it came up. It should have stopped him dead but he clung to my legs, clawing upwards. I put the gun against the side of his neck.

'Down,' I repeated.

He let go and flopped onto the carpet. I slapped handcuffs on him. One on his wrist, the other on his ankle. There was a chair in the corner and I stood it over him.

'If I see that so much as waggle,' I said, 'you'll lose your Christmas bonus.'

'Okay,' he said as though his teeth were cemented together. 'Okay.'

I sat in his chair and went through the desk drawers. The lightning stopped and the thunder rumbled away, leaving the rain lashing alone. As I shuffled and read the papers, that stopped too. I had four neat piles on the desk by the time dawn crept in around the blackout curtains. I leaned across the desk and banged on the chair-back.

'Where's the key to the safe?'

He grunted: 'What?'

'Wake up, sunshine,' I said. 'You been akip?' I went round and looked down at him. He craned his neck to look back, the whole right side of his jaw swollen.

'The safe keys,' I said, giving him a poke with my toe. All he did was grunt. 'Come on, there's nothing for you in holding out.'

'You've drawn a blank there, sailor. The owner keeps them on him. I don't handle a penny piece of cash.'

'That's too bad.'

'For you.'

'Not me. How would it be if I went and got my jelly from outside and used you for padding for the charge?'

'You what?' he said.

I looked at him. I looked at him a long time, and kept looking at him. He dropped his eyes.

'Back pocket,' he said.

I kneeled on his shoulders, flipped up his jacket and patted his backside. Something stood out from the flesh. I pulled out the key and used it. There was an address book and a book with names and amounts in neat columns, a banded roll of IOUs and a tin box with banknotes in. I left the tin box empty, and put everything else in the manager's briefcase.

'Up,' I said.

He rolled the chair off him and struggled up on one knee.

'What's Spandrell's number?'

He told me and I dialled it. When the burring started I put the receiver to his ear.

'When he answers, tell him you want him here as fast as he can. Make it sound important. But no details, right?'

He didn't get it. He just went through the motions.

'Hello ... Jackson here ... Yeah, the club ... no, I know he don't ... Yes I know what time it is ... Well would I if it wasn't important? ... I mean, would I? ...

Yes, get him ... Hello ... sorry, yeah ... Something's come up ... No ... I don't want to over the blower ... That's right ... Okay, if that's when you can ... Yeah, I'll be here ... Yeah.'

The burring started again. I put the phone back in its cradle.

'He said about eleven, I couldn't get him no faster. You don't push too hard.'

'You don't,' I said. 'Hold still.'

I sprang the cuff on his ankle and sat him back in his chair; pulled his arms behind the chair-back and locked his wrists together.

'What's your game?' he asked. 'You know he won't come here alone. He'll be team-handed. I don't get it.'

'You will if you don't keep shtum.'

I used his tie on his ankles, put a loop round them and up to the chain between the cuffs. With his feet off the ground he had no leverage. I slapped a strip of Elastoplast over his mouth. He watched me scatter files all over the floor, rip out the phone, and sweep everything off the desk onto the carpet. Then I picked up the briefcase and patted it.

'Tell him when he comes—this is for Ronny's widow.'

He didn't get that either. I left him sitting there trying to work it out.

Nine

I sat up on the roof watching the Sunday things going on in the street below. First, the clipped quietness of the early morning churchgoers; heads down and hurrying. The Hokey-Pokey man pedalling his 'Stop me and buy one' bicycle, calling out and ringing his bell. Then the Boy's Brigade drum and fife band, rolling and sharping through a hymn, smaller children skipping along the pavement to keep up. A hot potato man with his straw oven over his shoulder, throwing his spuds up to the windows that opened; catching the pennies that came back. Then the celery and whelk man trundling his barrow full of fresh and jellied eels, winkles and cockles, mussels, shrimps, rock salt and vinegar.

A lot later a black Daimler coasted into the street and turned into the club parking lot. All the doors opened and four men got out. They walked quickly to the side entrance.

I dropped back into the loft and sat looking down through the gap in the ladder bay. Feet banged up the stairs and a voice said:

'Jackson.'

The last time I'd heard that voice I was standing on a jetty with my arms up behind me and the Thames lapping over my shoes.

'If he's pulling my pudden on the one morning I get a lie-in, I'll have his tockers on the end of a sharp stick . . .'

Spandrell's voice died away, his feet rooted in the office doorway. The other shoes stood just as still. There was enough electricity in the air to light up Brighton Pier.

Then they all started talking at once; even the manager gobbled behind the plaster.

Spandrell walked into the office with all the shoes after him. There was a sharp ripping sound.

'Gawd, that hurt,' said the manager. 'Nearly took my lip off.'

There was the sound of a slap.

'Enough left for a right-hander,' said Spandrell. There was another slap. 'We've been turned over. Me. And all you can do is sit there complaining. Look at this place. Looks like a bloody bomb's hit it. How many was there?'

The manager didn't answer.

'You heard Mister Spandrell,' said Poncer. Paper crunched as he moved across the room.

'Watch your great plates on those files,' said Spandrell. 'Well?'

'One,' said the manager.

'You what?'

'One, a big bastard with a shooter. He had me cold on closing. Put his knee in me throat. I can still feel it when I swallow. I tell you, Spanner, he was all over me like lightning. Nothing I could do.'

'You chicken bastard. Who was he?'

'Search me. I never lamped him before. Not that I wouldn't know him again in a roomful. Big, like I said. Black hair, wears a trilby. Got a scar on his lip, makes his grin a bit crooked. Had a grey suit on and black shoes—looked all new. Oh yeah, and a bloody great cut on the back of his hand. The left one.'

'Anybody recognise a face like that?'

They must have all nodded their heads because nobody said a word.

'Put the bubble out,' said Spandrell. 'I want that bastard. It's worth five score to me. If that stuff gets in the hands of the busies we're all up the pictures with a ball and chain.'

Yelling came up the stairs and I caught sight of a bloke wearing an apron skid into the office.

'We're at war! At war, I tell you! Mister Chamberlain just give it out on the wireless. We're at war!'

There was a long holding of breath. Spandrell said:

'You're telling me.'

I went out onto the roof and lowered the skylight back into position, shot the bolts and tightened the nuts. When I'd finished you'd never have known it had been touched.

The city huddled under the bright high sky; silent and crisp in the sunlight. There didn't seem to be anybody alive anywhere. No traffic and no pedestrians. Even the pigeons hid in the trees under the motionless barrage balloons.

I went up the metal ladder over the chimney stack and down onto the next roof. Washing hung in rows, still in the windless air. A wireless blared from a window below the parapet, wheezing out the National Anthem. It clicked off as I went down the fire escape and climbed into the back window of the flat I'd rented.

Then came a wail, starting somewhere over the rooftops towards Westminster, rolling over the roofs and echoing through the streets. Sirens began all over the city. The first alert of the war. A baby began to cry in sympathy, cutting through the walls as though they weren't there. It was eleven twenty-seven.

Manny answered at the first ring.

'You heard the news?' I said.

'So it's about time they woke up. Took 'em long enough. You should hear some of what I've heard from the poor nebishes I met from Czechoslovakia. They could tell you tales.'

'Doesn't anything surprise you?' I said.

'What's to surprise? How about you do it and tell me what you got?'

'All the stuff from the safe and a lot of papers from

the files. You'll have to go through most of it, I'm no bloody clerk.'

An aeroplane, a fighter I think, went over low, rattling the tiles. The roar covered what Manny said next.

'What?'

'It doesn't matter. Bring the stuff by when you're ready. Some of it could make a nice Monday post for the law.'

'Too previous, Manny my son. I want them sweating for a good long bit. As long as I can stretch it. When I'm ready I'll give it to a certain copper in person. That'll be a perk. Anyway, there's a lot of due IOUs that could use collecting. Grands of them. They'll keep me in rent money for a couple of Christmases. You want the banker's split? The usual fifteen per cent?'

'I want it,' said Manny so softly I could almost hear him doing his slow and sad satisfied nod.

'And to save you asking,' I said, 'I'll be careful collecting on 'em. They're spread half round London anyway. It'd take all Spanner's got to keep all them drums under his minces.'

'You say,' said Manny. 'So you say. Suit yourself. Make it round here after dark, with the blackout it should be safe enough. I know a couple of geezers who've made a bundle sandbagging the odd punter in the dark. There's a lot of fat wallets about, though handbags is easier.'

'Don't tell me about lice like that. It don't sit right in my book to knock old tarts about for their few coppers.'

'Who's condoning? I meet all sorts. If I had your conscience I'd be boracic in minutes. Anyway, teddah, I got things to organise. I've got a warehouse full of torches to place and a face to see about the batteries to go with them.'

'When was that turned over?'

'Tonight. Should be all right if those bleeding blackout wardens don't get to nosing about.'

'A couple of old dads in tin hats. Shout boo and they'll wet themselves.'

'You wish. Teddah,' said Manny and rang off. I stripped off and climbed into bed and was asleep before the all-clear sounded.

There was a ridiculous quiet over everything like a fine dust when I woke up. No light showed through the dark windows, no glow of street lighting, no searchlights. Just dark and quiet. My watch ticked like a woodpecker chewing on a gong. I got up, put the blackout board up at the window and turned on the light. There wasn't much to see in the room, just the folding bed, a chair with half the stuffing hanging out and a suitcase alongside the old steamer trunk I kept my clothes in. The walls were cream and the lino was a vicious blue with worn brown patches. The bulb hung on the end of its wire like a fly-specked corpse. It threw shadows everywhere.

I went through into the kitchen, which was equally crummy. There was a gas oven, a sink with a cold tap and a wooden draining board with a cup and a plate on it, a chair and a card table that had lost its baize covering. I couldn't see me defending my home and hearth against the Nazi hordes. I boiled a kettle, used the water to make a cup of tea and shaved. I was dressed and out in the street in five minutes.

In the street it seemed darker, the buildings cutting into the hard black sky; blacker black on black. I went along the railings, feeling my way to the local on the corner.

The interior was a jigsaw of flickering light and shade from the half-dozen candles stuck around the place. I got myself a pint and sat up at the bar with it. Everybody was talking in whispers except for an old biddy and her tarty mate in the corner. They chatted away, swallowing stout as though tonight was the last one.

'I ain't going nowhere but home after this. Blimey, it's bad enough round here with the lights going, without all this dark. I tell you it's unnerving,' said the tart.

The old lady looked like she was made of crumpled cardboard, her head shaking as she listened.

'Nothing,' she said, 'this is nothing like the last lot. My Bill, Gawd bless him, never came back from Flanders. I had to get along with rationing and everything. They ain't said nothing about that, have they? No, Vera, they haven't. Won't, neither. Take my word, it won't last till Christmas, you take my word.'

Vera's face was a white blank around her red slash of a mouth.

'Course, if they do,' said the old lady. 'I mean, talk about rationing and that, take my word. You stock yourself up with sugar and tea. And butter and elastic. That goes first. The ships, you see.'

'Where am I gonna get money for butter?' asked Vera. 'Marge is what I can go to, and marge is all I can go to. Talk sense, Gran. Can you see my Charlie giving me anything for extras? Takes all his time to part with enough to get us through the week. I tell you, they'd do me a favour if they had him off in the army on this conscription lark.'

'That's wicked and you know it,' said the old lady sharply.

'How is it? When he's boozing life's no comedy, I can tell you.'

'He'll settle down.'

'In a thousand years.'

They went moody and quiet, holding their empty glasses, both hoping the other was buying the next. I lit up a cigarette and offered one to the bloke behind the bar. He said 'Ta' and sucked the smoke down hard.

'You in for anything?' he said.

'No.'

'I been doing ARP training since the summer. You know, gas training and that. It puts the wind up you, you know? Not like for me, the old woman and the kids.

I got masks for her and the eldest, but they got nothing out for the baby yet. I mean, what happens to her if it happens?'

'Pray it don't,' I said.

'Maybe you're right,' he said.

'I hope so.'

'They took my brother for the reservists this afternoon, got him off at five minutes notice. The old mother's in a rare old state about it.'

I made a non-committal noise. The old lady said:

'We had the zeppelins, you know. Used to be up there for hours, dropping bombs. Hard, that was. This generation couldn't stand up to that, I can tell you. Cut of cheaper cloth nowadays.'

Vera folded over and started to cry. Long racking sobs. The old lady looked at her with as much surprise on her face as a badly-wrapped parcel.

'Gawd, girl,' she muttered, 'you can't half turn it on.'

'I'm sorry,' said Vera. 'Sorr-ree.' It was all she could manage. She bowed over with her face in shadow under her peroxide hair.

'Why the Dracula lighting?' I asked the barman.

'I've had a barney with the brewery for months about proper blackout. I've only got black paper up the windows and the top lights are too strong for it. The warden's a mouthy pusher at the best of times; a pledge merchant too. He's just waiting to have a go.'

'There's a lot round like it,' I said.

'Another one?'

I pushed my mug at him and he went off to the pumps in the gloom.

'Come on, girl,' said the old lady.

'I can't. I got to evacuate the kids. They're on the train Tuesday. They can't even tell us where they're going, not proper. Just said Gloucestershire or some such.'

'What, the kids? That ain't right.'

'It's the whole school's going. All of them together on the train,' mumbled Vera. The old lady mumbled back, pawing at Vera's shoulder with rough sympathy. I got my second pint and downed half of it in one. The barman took the money and went along the bar, tapping his optics on his way to the till. I looked along the shelves at the labels and the advertising flotsam.

There was a stand-up Player's display, a colour drawing of two yachting enthusiasts on a foreshore with gulls and a white sail in the background, one had a yachting cap and a pipe, the other had a cigarette and a woollen bobble hat; both had very white teeth. They grinned across at a wooden Johnny Walker striding along the shelf between a bottle of Green Goddess and a Guinness Ostrich. Vera breathed jerkily and the barman blew smoke up at the ceiling. The shadows were filled with the shock of it all. I drank the rest of my beer and went out.

The streets were just as quiet and just as hushed as before. A car went past with no lights showing, its wheel right in the kerb. I crossed the road behind it and went down the back doubles towards Stoke Newington. I lost count of the walls I bounced off and the people that I bumped into. As I turned into Newington Green I half sprawled over a man crouching up near a garden wall.

'Sorry, mate,' he said.

'All right.'

'I was just trying to see where I was from this road sign. I can't even read it with me nose right up against it.'

'You live round here?' I asked.

'All me born natural. I got a cab at the kerb. I tell you, it ain't worth coming out nights when you can't use even your sidelights. I've bashed up a wing already.'

'Light a match, why don't you?'

'I tried that. I had a bloody copper breathing all over me. He's took me number and everything. Reckons I'll get summonsed for it.'

'Bastards.'

'Not half,' he said with feeling.

Manny shuffled down the passage after I'd knocked twice. No light showed through the half-glazed door. A bolt slid along its track, another clicked, and a couple of chains chinked. Something wasn't right. His head came round the door, an oily blob in the night.

'Yes,' he said.

'Manny.'

'Hallo, Jack boy, what's on?' he asked.

I looked past him into the dark hall, and could just see that the front room door was half open.

'Hello, Manny. I got you the tickets you wanted. Two dozen, weren't it?' I half shouted, then, in a whisper, 'Company?'

'Yeah. I thought you'd come a lot sooner.' His voice dropped. 'Two,' he said. 'Poncer and Jacko.'

'Couldn't get away. The missus was playing up. You know how they are when they're in the last month.'

'Hand 'em over.'

I slid past him and went up the hall past the open door.

'Thanks, Jack boy. I'll get the poppy tomorrow,' Manny said to the empty area. 'Teddah.' He took his time with the bolts and the chains. He dropped the blackout blind over the door and the light went on. Poncer leaned out into the passage with his back to me, busy looking at Manny's bruised old face.

'Good,' he said. 'You done good there. Inside here.' He jerked his thumb at the front room. Manny stayed where he was and folded his arms across his fairisle pull-over.

'So you can use the hose on me again? What for, I told you there's nothing to tell.'

'You say,' said Poncer, 'so you say. Don't tell me I got to come and get you in here. That what's wanted?'

If there's such a thing as a Jewish bulldog, Manny was

it. His head was a mass of lumps, and there was a red line down his temple. The lines down the sides of his mouth looked like they'd been drawn with black crayon.

'Go home, Poncer. There's nothing here for you. Nothing.'

Poncer laughed: 'Hear that, Jacko? He's put out with us for giving him a tickling. He'll be calling the law next.'

'Get him in here. We ain't got all night to fart about with the old get. There's other calls to make.'

Poncer slapped his palm with the cosh.

'You heard what Jacko said.'

Manny slowly worked his mouth and spat on the floor.

Poncer came all the way out into the hall, the cosh coming back over his shoulder at me. I caught his wrist and pulled him back and round, bringing my knee up into his gut. He made a noise with his eyes all the way open. I ripped the cosh away and let him have one stroke to the middle of his forehead, a solid one that banged his head into the wall. Another one shut his eyes and straightened him out on the lino.

Manny started yelling like he had ants all over him.

'What's the game?' called Jacko. 'Shut the old pill up.'

'You try some,' I called.

'One old man and you're euchred. That's your mark all over,' said Jacko coming out in a hurry. Manny began a dance to go with the yelling. Jacko's foot caught in Poncer's side and he half-sprawled with his hands slapping on the passage walls, going away from me. I gave him one on the shoulder, not hard enough to stop him. He yelled and forced himself up, sliding against the wall. There was a click as his spring-blade opened and he lunged; an upward movement using all his arm. The blade ran up through my lapel and parted the hair at my temple, spraying plaster as it hit the wall. He was over me like a blanket, both of us trampling Poncer.

We spun down the hall like heavyweight tango

champions, grunting and heaving. He was strong and he smelled sour. We cannoned into the broom cupboard, splintering the door and rolling in on the stored junk. Glass tinkled and something made of wood squealed into pieces as we both hit the floor. The knife suddenly wasn't there any more and Jacko's hand left my wrist. I smashed at him with the cosh, short blows and rapid, with his hands trying to grab at me. After a bit they just waved and then went limp. Then he was limp all over with only his breathing moving his chest.

'What do we do with them?' said Manny.

I just stayed where I was, heaving in great gulps of Jacko's body odour and the smell of damp. Manny repeated himself.

'How do I know?' I said. 'It's like a bloody coalmine outside. The streets are stiff with busies and wardens, and no cars can show any lights. We wouldn't get fifty yards without getting lost or having a bang. That'd be lovely with two burkes in the back with known faces.'

Manny kicked Poncer in the side. He muttered something in the back of his throat. I got the meaning, whatever language it was he used.

'I hope you feel better.'

'Better is right,' Manny said, and did it again. He was wearing carpet slippers. Jacko started to snore. I'd seen drawings in the *Beano* do it but I thought it was just a joke. It isn't.

'We just lock them in the lav, do we, that's what we do?'

I got up without answering, brushing the fluff and filth off me. My lapel flapped.

'Look at that, will you? Seven and a half quid this suit set me back. I'll have it out of his wallet,' I said. Manny went down and did the honours.

'A oncer, half a quid and a pawn ticket. You'll be lucky.' He flicked the piece of green card at me. I let it hit the floor.

'Kick him again, the cheap toerag. Then help me drag him through into the back room. We'll stack them there.'

'You barmy? For why? Until daylight maybe, then drop them off in a refuse dump somewhere.'

'They stay there. Permanent. I don't give a monkey's if they're not found till the stormtroopers land. I mean, this residence is desirable enough to make Gestapo Headquarters.'

'A joke that ain't. Where do I go? Berlin, maybe?'

'There's places. A couple I can think of right off. Come on, let's get gone out of it.'

Manny got up with grey-white rounds on his trousers.

'Go, just go. Just like that? Twenty years I been here. Twenty years. You don't just wipe it out with a "let's go". There's things...'

I interrupted. 'Three rooms and a bog in the garden that freezes your arse off in the summer even. Distempered walls and boards you can put your foot through on tiptoe. Leave out the hearts and sodding flowers. You stay here and you'll have to top those two and post little bits of 'em over the country, or they'll cut your heart out with the nearest potato peeler. There's no time. We go, or...'

I picked up Jacko's knife and slapped it into Manny's palm.

'...cut them now. Go on, I ain't doing it for you.'

Manny looked down at the knife as though it was sticking in his own stomach. He used his other hand to scrub the top of his head.

'Why now?' he asked. 'If it happened another time, they'd be in the river long since. But now...' He made an expressive gesture with his shoulders and let the knife drop point first into the lino.

'Now,' I said. 'There's no way to dump them. You can't get an ear on the other end of the blower that'll listen to a topping job, not even for half a grand.'

'I'll get some rope,' said Manny. I lifted Jacko by the

'That's all right then. I'll see you.'

'Hang about...'

I rang off. Manny was in an overcoat that could have been worn at Gallipoli, a balaclava over his head. The suitcase looked heavy and was held shut with a couple of straps.

'What do you look like?' I said.

'When do I go out? A fashion show you need maybe?'

We went out and locked the door before going up the area steps into the street and off through the dark and quiet.

Ten

After a lot of knocking a window went up on the top floor and a smudge of a head looked out.

'Who is it?' said a light girl's voice.

'Me,' I said.

'Who the hell's me?'

'Bergie.'

She made a breathy sort of squeal and said:

'I might have known. Wait until I get down there, waking up the whole street with your banging and bawling.'

The window slid down, stuck, went up a bit, then closed with a shudder.

'Hey, Bergie,' said Manny urgently, 'look.'

I went cold squinting up and down the road for movement.

'No, up there.'

The sky was a painful black behind the plough's hard-etched formation.

'I've never seen the sky so clear. Not ever.' Manny was like a kid in front of Selfridge's Christmas display.

'You burke. You scared the beGod out of me.'

'Makes me feel small,' he whispered.

'What, in that overcoat?'

Feet padded on the stairs and along the hall and the door swung open. I stepped through with Manny coming reluctantly.

'Who's this?' said the girl.

'Have you seen the sky, miss? You can almost touch the stars.'

'Have I what? At this time of the night, when all decent people are well asleep in their beds? Keep your voice down, can't you, there'll be a rucking if you wakes the old lady up. I don't know I should be letting you in anyway.'

'It's you that's doing most of the talking anyway,' I said. 'Come on, let's get upstairs out of this draught. You'll catch your death.'

I slapped her bottom lightly and felt her warm buttocks through the worn dressing gown. It was red when you could see it. She slapped my hand away and went off up the stairs after putting her finger up to her lips.

Her room was small and neat. The wallpaper couldn't have been more than a year old. There was a single bed with rumpled blankets and a single depression in the pillow. A sideboard with two dolls and a threadbare teddy sitting beside a hairbrush and a lot of bottles and little boxes, a film of facepowder over them. A wardrobe with a mirrored centre and a hard chair with clothes over the back.

She stood with her back against the bed and chewed her lip. She was small and thin-faced with light auburn hair, slightly mussed from sleeping.

Her face shone with cold cream and her generous mouth was free of lipstick. Her eyes were grey with heavy lashes.

'Hello, Doreen love,' I said.

'Don't you Doreen me,' she hissed. 'You been out going on two months and not even a penny card. You wouldn't even let me come on visiting days.'

She would have gone on but I said, 'Not in front of company, Dee.'

She looked round me at Manny with her nose wrinkled. I didn't blame her. He did look like a refugee from Transylvania.

'We need a drum for the night. We'll be gone in the morning. I wouldn't ask, but...'

'Go on. That's familiar. Well, I don't see why I should bother.'

'Nor do I.'

'You gaily walk in here after two years and want putting up...'

'You're right.'

'Not so much as a by-your-leave...'

'We'll go. You've made your point.'

'What's up with his face?'

'Thanks anyway.'

'What happened to his face?'

'His bunny bit him.'

'Some bloody bunny,' she shot me a shrewd look. 'It's started up again, hasn't it? No, don't tell me, I know. He can have the camp bed next door, and you can get comfortable on the lino. I don't know why I bother.'

She pushed past me, grabbed Manny and took him off making mothering noises at him. I lit a cigarette and sat on the edge of the bed until she came back. She wasn't long.

'I've told him no lights. There's no blackout in there and he'll have to get comfortable in the dark. He looks worn out, poor old bleeder. I knew him as soon as he had that balaclava off. Did I ever tell you what we did as kids when he give us sweets in the market?'

'You don't have to,' I said.

She walked around to the other side of the bed and tucked her feet under the clothes. She took a cigarette from my packet and let me light it for her. We sat looking at each other through the smoke. She could hardly hold the cigarette for shaking.

'Cold?' I said.

She shook her head.

'You may as well let me have it and get it over,' I offered.

Something like a smile moved her lips. Gone almost as soon as it showed.

'Would it do any good?'

'No.'

'No,' she said.

'How've you been?'

'So-so. Up and down. I haven't slept well since you went running off that night straight into the cells. I was in court.'

'I didn't see you.'

'You didn't see anybody. You looked dead.' She sniffled and was suddenly crying without changing her expression. I reached out and took up one of the tears on the end of a finger, putting it to my lips.

'It's nice to have someone cry for me,' I said.

She grabbed my hand and pressed it against her face, pecking kisses at the palm. I was startled without knowing why. Maybe being alone for so long. Maybe having one pair of legs in my bed for so long did it, I don't know. I just sat there with my leg going to sleep, stiff and feeling awkward.

'Don't, Dee,' I said with a mouthful of dried peas. 'Don't take on.'

She smelled of bed-warmth and cheap powder and her nose was red. I took her cigarette and mine and dropped both of them into the ashtray by my foot, reaching out and stroking her hair. She slipped sideways into my lap, pressing her mouth up onto mine. Her mouth tasted of lipstick and salt, quivering and cool.

Her hand found mine, thrusting it deep inside her dressing gown and onto her breast. It burned in my hand, soft against the callouses, the crest hardened. There wasn't any gentleness from then on. I was as rampant as a Queen's beast as I stripped off her gown and bit into her. She wasn't any softer about it. It couldn't have taken much longer than it took Manny to climb out of his overcoat. Short, savage and very sweet.

We smoked afterwards. Smoked and whispered. I got

undressed properly and got right in beside her, her legs curled up across me, her face on my chest. We talked old times and pictures we'd sat through together in the back row, holding hands as other couples writhed around us.

'It's all changed now, though,' she said.

'You mean this war?'

'Yeah,' she said, nibbling my pectoral. 'They've moved out next door. Me and the old lady are off tomorrow. We're going down to the hopping fields. It's about the right time, and we'll be out of it for a while. I don't reckon myself in a gas mask. Gran insists we take them.'

'That sounds like her.'

'What'll you do? I mean, there's a lot talking of joining up.'

'Not this kiddy. They've had two years out of me, and that's all they'll get.'

'You ain't the old laughing Bergie, are you? I can feel you go hard when you think about it. Relax, can't you? It's like being in bed with a sheet of corrugated iron. Get any sharper and you'll tear the sheets.'

'I heard you had a bloke,' I said into her hair.

'I went out a couple of times. He was nice. A gentleman. Never touched me or nothing.'

'Oh yeah.'

'Yes,' she said, slapping me. 'Honest, if they don't grope you think they're fairies. He wasn't anything like that. He was just ... nice.'

'Then there's nothing to tell.'

'He wanted to marry me.'

'Why didn't he?'

'You know why. And if you don't you're barmy.'

'You should have done, he'd have got you out of all this.'

She was quiet for a bit, her hands running along my thigh and across my stomach.

'You're like iron,' she said.

'I will be if you keep that up.'

'What a lovely idea.'

'Well, why didn't you?'

She sighed, her hand kneading me with more and more urgency.

'Well?' I said. She slid down across me with her mouth coming onto mine.

'You talk too much,' she said.

She was right.

I was up and dressed as the window turned grey. She was asleep on her face, hair tumbled across the pillow, strands of it stirring from her breath. I left a couple of fivers tucked into teddy's bow and let myself out. Manny was sitting with his suitcase across his lap when I went into his room.

'That's a nice girl,' he said. 'Not many like that.'

'She'll do.'

He caught my sleeve and held it, saying:

'A girl like that is worth something. You should feel lucky. For a gargoyle like me, money has to be passed.'

'I'm lucky, Manny. All right? Now let's get gone before the streets get busy. That's what's called making your own luck.'

We went down the stairs with him muttering in my ear. Outside it was a grey morning, the air chilled and misty. The first Monday of the war. We stepped out through the thickening streams of workers on their way to graft for three pounds ten a week and the chance of a bit more on overtime. A billposter was sticking up red and white posters on a hoarding. They all said:

FREEDOM IS IN PERIL

DEFEND IT WITH ALL YOUR MIGHT

The dole queue on the other side of the road catcalled and yelled obscene suggestions as to what the bloke could do with his broom. The back of his neck was as red as the posters. He posted the last one a bit wonky and cycled off without hanging about. A warden coming in the opposite direction was given much the same treatment.

'Notice something?' said Manny.

'No.'

'Take a look around. They're all looking up. All of them, now and again they take a squint at the sky and then dig their chins into their collars.'

'Yeah, you can smell the fear coming up out of the pavement.' I grabbed Manny's arm and we crossed the intersection, stopping on the centre refuge. A lot of the traffic was ignoring the signals. There were private cars piled with luggage, lorries stacked with the corrugated sections used for Anderson shelters and packed with sallow-faced workmen.

A charabanc rolled past full of singing schoolchildren with labels around their necks, a flustered-looking woman teacher conducting from beside the driver. They cheered and waved as they passed us. Manny set his precious case down and waved back.

'Look at that, Bergie. Kids. Full of life and fight,' he said.

'Pick up your case. We'll get across after this next one.'

Manny stayed where he was.

'No, boy.'

'Whatcha mean, no?'

'I'm going back. There's no running away.'

'Who's running, for crying out loud?'

'I was. You go, I'll be all right.'

'Manny, this ain't the time or place.'

'It'll do. Teddah, boy. Stay in touch. And good luck to you.'

'Manny, will you come on?'

Manny smiled his sad smile and ducked for his case, turning to look across the other stream of traffic for a hole.

'Manny.'

I was talking to his back. He was off between a bus and a car and shuffling along the pavement. He turned and gave a sharp wave. A dismissing gesture. It was then I noticed he was still in his carpet slippers.

'Here, mate!'

I looked up at a driver of a charabanc. He was sweating under his peaked cap, looking lost.

'Yeah?'

'All right for Liverpool Street Station?'

He was carrying a girls' school from South London. The girls were in quiet uniformed rows looking out at the jammed crossroads with solemn boredom. The teacher in charge was knitting.

'Straight on,' I said. 'Turn right at the next lot of lights.'

'Thanks a lot. Bloody mess, ain't it?'

He grinned and winked and engaged his gears and roared away.

'A bloody mess,' I said to his tail light.

I got across the road and found an empty phone booth, thumbed in the money and dialled Whitehall one two, one two.

'Hello, Mister Lemmon,' I said when I got through to him.

'Hello, chummy. You're hardly a welcome follow-up to a good breakfast. Are you coming in to face the charges for assaulting a policeman, or have I got to come and get you?'

'You bloody prove it first. I wasn't in any fit state and you know a jury would see it my way. Anyway, you must have found a sleeping face in the grounds. Not that you kept him long.'

'Laurie Naismith can wait. We found him face down like you say, says he was attacked and robbed and asked what we were going to do about it. Even found himself a solicitor to help him out.'

'Forget him. There's something that could use your personal touch; a couple of faces at Manny's place. Breaking and entering should do it. But you'll have to be quick.'

'Wouldn't be two of Spanner's, by some coincidence? Lost their way?'

'You want them or don't you?'

'Not half as much as another.'

'Him you won't get on a plate. Just get down there, will you?'

'Asking a favour, Bergman? Try saying please.'

'Not for a pension. Get there in ten minutes and you could save a topping. That's worth getting off your backside for.'

Lemmon's voice sharpened. 'You spieling or is that God's truth? Come on, spit it out or swallow.'

'Straight as the crease in your trousers. You've got nine minutes—maybe!'

I banged the phone down and a sweat-ball burst on the back of my hand. My reflection in the mirror beside the emergency instructions was yellow and wet, purple shadows under the eyes. I pressed Button B automatically. It chattered without any coins dropping. I lit a fag and waited. A woman opened the door and asked how long I was going to be. I told her I was waiting for a call from my sister in Durham to tell me my kids had got off the train safely. She clucked and went away.

I let minutes roll by slower than the traffic, then dialled again. Lemmon was out of his office and he wasn't expected back for at least an hour. I said I'd call back later, left a fictitious name and rang off.

'You've got a chance, Manny,' I said to my reflection. 'A bloody good one.'

Eleven

The winter came in hard. It got right in among the trees as they were turning brown and gold for their autumn show. The leaves went black and fell off into the frost and ice covering the public parks. It rained and sleeted and snowed and got colder and colder. The air-raid trenches filled with water and froze up. The pipes in my flat froze and thawed and burst and froze and burst again. The plumbers did good business and the sparrows froze in the trees. The old lady in the flat under me froze to death in front of an empty grate.

The Government rationed bacon, ham and butter, combined all the brands of petrol as 'Pool' and sold it at one and six a gallon. A lot of families had butter on the table for the first time in their lives. They were entitled to a ration, so they wanted it. There was a lot of hoarding going on. Rich old tarts drove out to West Ham and Stepney to buy up stuff in bulk. It's hard to stand by and watch your local shop get emptied by strangers with toffee accents and more than the three-ha'pence.

Theatres and cinemas closed for a bit, then opened again. Dog-racing meetings were held in the afternoons and the West End closed early and stayed unlit.

The snow hit the railways hard. Trains were days late instead of hours. Milk froze on the doorsteps and more than once I had to break the bottle to get at it. A lot of people got fed up being evacuated and went back home. They slid back into their slums as if they'd never been away. They grumbled and gossiped as much as before and they learned to queue. They queued for bread and outside the butchers. They formed lines at bus stops and only pushed and shoved when the buses pulled in. The war seemed a long way off. All we had were shortages.

The Merchant Navy was getting hammered by the U-boats and the Royal Navy cruised up and down looking for someone to fight. A lot of fighting was going on in places I'd never heard of. I wasn't the only one. No German planes came near the balloons over London and people stopped looking up except to see if it was raining. A lot of the time it was.

Hotels out in the West Country, a 'Safe Zone', filled up with more rich old biddies with nails too long to wash up with. They drank the bars dry, knitting the odd things for soldiers in their spare time. A lot of schools and church halls were commandeered for use as Civil Defence posts and the WVS got busy with the poor sods with less than nothing. They had their hands full. There were one million six hundred thousand unemployed.

Anderson shelters were shoved up in most back gardens and the AFS spent most of its time pumping them out. More long-winded propaganda posters went up on hoardings and shop fronts. Nobody read them.

Everybody was issued with gas masks and the Lost Property offices filled up with them. Not one word about the bitterest winter in living memory was allowed to be printed. According to the papers there was no weather at all.

The pubs and factories were full of chat about the invasion and scares about fifth columnists. Barriers went up on the South Coast beaches and some seaside towns were deserted and left to the gulls. Street shelters were built but it was the kids that damaged them instead of the Luftwaffe. The London Underground was banned for use as a shelter during alerts. That didn't stop anybody. They bought tickets and went down anyway. It was a time of waiting and trying to keep warm, a time of going without.

The spring came and ended the waiting. Hitler invaded Norway and Denmark. Before the last crocus had withered the British Expeditionary Force was shunted onto the beaches of Dunkirk. As far as I was concerned it was just another bloody nose in a series of bloody noses. It was in the newspapers, bold black headlines under the Friday night fish and chips, soaked in vinegar and covered with salt. That's if the chip shop got its delivery; most of the fishing fleet was sweeping mines instead of trawling.

It got warmer and turned into a great summer. The skies were blue and the sun was hot. People started looking up again and using their shelters. By the end of August they weren't bothering.

Twelve

It was one of those big Victorian houses that lay back off the road with its own scoop drive facing Hampstead Heath. It must have taken the output of a whole cloth factory to black out the windows. I crunched up the gravel past the flowering shrubs and rhododendrons, the cherub pouring nothing from his horn of plenty into a drained pool, the overgrown grass borders. I guessed the gardener had been called up.

I swung on the bell pull and ringing came from forty rooms away. Hard heels clacked on parquet and the door swung in for the butler to look out. His head was far enough back for me to see the linings of his nostrils. He was wearing the whole traditional lot, high collar, dickie bow, striped waistcoat and black tailcoat. Undressed he would have been just a fat man.

'Yes,' he said, making it sound like no.

'I'm expected,' I said.

'Yes?'

I showed him the address written on the card with Hymie's name at the top. He put his hand out for it but I moved it out of his reach. 'Wait,' he said as he began to close the door. I blocked it open with my foot. We wrestled a bit, with the door coming off worst.

'You will wait here.'

'Inside, cocker. There's a right George Raft up me kilt.'

He threw open the door and stuck his stomach out at me, hissing:

'What's your game? Another peep and I'll have the chauffeur bounce you down the path on your jaxie.'

'That'd make a lot of noise. You want to chance it? Specially when your gaffer's dead keen to see me.'

'What, you?'

'Me.'

He looked behind him with yellow eyeballs.

'All right! But just inside. I don't want you wandering or so help me it's Hampstead nick for you.'

'What I want'll be handed to me voluntary.'

'Step inside, sir. I'll see if the master's at home.'

He switched accents like a ventriloquist.

The hall was the size of the average church nave, all panelled wood with swords and shields and old flintlocks in lines and circles. Paintings too, military stuff in heavy gilt frames, brave red squares up against the dreaded dervish.

'There,' he said, pointing to a wooden grapevine with four legs that could have been a chair. It stood between two glass cabinets cluttered with china General Gordons and Dukes of Wellington. The china sparkled, the gilt shone and the oiled wood gleamed. You could have eaten your dinner off the floor.

The butler gave me another warning look and padded off to scratch on some double doors off to the side. He went inside, only using one door. He was gone long enough for me to want a smoke. There weren't any ash-trays so I just watched the Scots Greys ploughing into the French guns with their sabres flashing in the watery sunlight. Even the wounded were posed and heroic. I crossed my legs, uncrossed them, crossed them again and folded my arms. The grapes and leaves cut into me whichever way I sat.

The butler opened both the doors coming out, leaving them open. He used two fingers to lever me out of the chair. It seemed to take forever to get down that hall to where he stood. He gave me a pink look as I winked and went past him. He snicked the doors closed behind me.

The room was as big as I thought it would be, which was surprising. It had more books in it than Hackney Public Library, in rows right up to the ceiling, with a ladder that slid round on a brass rail. There was a reading desk and a lectern under windows that looked out on a miniature version of Sherwood Forest. But then maybe Sherwood Forest wasn't as big as I thought. There was a Persian rug in the middle of the room with a chesterfield standing on it. On the chesterfield sat a man in a blue mess jacket smoking a cigar in a holder.

He was long-legged and thin-chested. His hands and fingers were slender with huge knuckles. He had a military brush under his Plantagenet nose, pouched eyes with brown pupils and grey flashes over his ears. He didn't get up or move. I wasn't sure he was even looking at me. He was holding a slim volume.

'Are you familiar with Liddell-Hart's writings, Mister...?'

He let the end of the sentence go with his eyebrows up.

'No.'

'Fascinating. Good solid stuff. The Germans, I fear, have taken his Blitzkrieg theories to heart—more than our chaps have. Tragedy.'

His voice was as rich as Christmas cake. I didn't know what he was talking about and he knew it.

'Poland and Norway, it's all there if you want to see it.'

'Very interesting,' I said. 'D'you mind if I smoke?'

'Feel free.'

I said thanks and lit up as he carefully bookmarked his place, snapping the covers together. He straightened his legs and grew upwards to a good six foot six. When he had tucked the little book away on a shelf he leaned on the lectern.

'Your telephone call intrigued me, Mister whatever

your name is. An IOU, you said. Bearing my name. The sum involved being . . .' He waved his arm behind him as though he were conducting a mouse orchestra.

I blew smoke and said, 'Four hundred and seventy-five quid.'

'Yes. Quite so. A great deal of money. Especially . . .' he let that word hang too, as if he liked the taste of it, '. . . especially since I have not gambled since I was a very young man. Does that set you thinking, perhaps?'

'Maybe.'

'Only maybe.' He sounded surprised.

'Maybe, like I said.'

'Maybe.' He said it as though it tasted bad. I let him taste while I strolled about looking for an ashtray. There was a brass dish by the fireplace filled with sand, a crushed cigar in it with its chewed tail in the air. I flicked my Woodbine ash beside it.

'Yours isn't a military family. Not even other ranks.'

'No. My family isn't even a family.'

'No.'

'No.'

'No traditions, codes of behaviour. That sort of thing.'

'Nothing that you'd recognise as anything like. It's mostly number one first in my manor.'

'Quite so, quite so,' he said, as though confirming something in his own mind. 'Then,' he added, 'you couldn't be expected to understand.'

I was getting dizzy.

'Look,' I said, 'I came here with a deal that you either want or you don't. It don't matter a monkey's to me if it was your old mother who'd done the family fortune or the housekeeping in on a herd of slow ponies, all I need to know is do you want to redeem, or don't you?'

'I don't,' he said.

'Fair enough. It can go back where it came from and you can pay at the full rate. A pity, that. They won't be patient like I am.'

I started for the door.

'I don't want to come to an arrangement with you. But...'

I stopped with my hand on the brass boar that opened the lock.

'But,' he said, 'it seems that honour dictates I must.'

I turned towards him.

'Honour? I've heard of debts of that stuff, but straight I didn't expect nothing like that with a geezer like Hymie the bookie.'

It was like talking to somebody from a Flash Gordon flick. His face was calm and thin and turned towards me. So was the service revolver in his long hand.

'And you won the shooting cup for the bloody regiment, I suppose. You'd use that to save yourself a few hundred quid. You must be dead mean. Half a dozen of them china soldiers out there would cover it. Leave more room to dust as well. That means I'm doing you a favour.'

I tried to talk slowly but it came out faster and faster.

'Just sit down,' he ordered. I sat down. He lowered himself onto the chesterfield with the elbow under his gun resting on his knee.

'I should like to see the document.' Then, 'Thank you,' when I handed it across.

'You realise that this isn't my signature,' he said.

'It's somebody's.'

'My son's.'

'Is it?'

'Without a doubt. I've seen a great many in my time.'

'Wild oats,' I said. I'd stopped pumping sweat but my heart was banging out a Cuban marimba.

'You could say that. Yes. Well, you might. This,' he waved the IOU, 'is dated September of last year, I really thought that I'd got them all in. I burned them all on Christmas Day. A present to myself.'

I watched him talk. He had the gun and it was his house.

'There were quite a few of these. They made quite a blaze. You mentioned twenty-five per cent of the face value?'

'Yes.'

'That is exactly...'

I finished for him.

'One hundred and seventeen quid.'

'And ten shillings.'

'We can forget that,' I said with a big wave of my hand.

'No.' His voice was sharp for the first time. 'No, we cannot.' He threw me a bundle of new banknotes. 'Count them, if you please. I want you to agree that the amount asked for is there.'

I counted them. Right down to the ten-bob note.

'Dead right,' I said. Now I was really confused. I held up the wad like a blue fan.

'Put it away in your pocket. I'm sure I don't need this now.'

He flopped the gun on the end of the couch.

'You never did.'

'Perhaps. I just wanted to see what sort of creature you were. It would have been most unpleasant if you had squirmed like some of them I've had to deal with. I had one grovelling on the carpet. I shot him.'

'Do what?'

'Oh, it was a blank. The fellow puked.'

'Did he.'

'I quite enjoyed it until I caught a gleam of reproach in my batman's eye. The carpet, you know.'

I nodded to let him know he still had my full attention and thought of the poor bastard of a collector choking over the Persian under my feet. It did nothing to cheer me up.

'My son was a bright lad. But lazy. Regular Army, joined the regiment for me. Did well, then he just went to pieces. Drinking and so on. Bit of a mess really. Still, that's history now. Killed in France.'

'Sorry,' I said, and meant it.

'I don't want a sorry from you. I've got all you can hand me, bought and paid for. This grubby piece of paper. Stolen by you, obviously. My son ... died in a driving accident. He was drunk. He killed the other fellow with him. And two girls. Tarts, I suppose, but that doesn't change anything. And it doesn't excuse a fellow like you whoring from your betters when ...'

I made the long journey to my feet and stood looking down at the top of his head as he looked at the IOU. Somehow my voice came out quiet.

'Say what you like, Colonel, I usually tell people I'm too ignorant to be insulted; usually am, too. I am sorry about your boy. More, as it happens, now I know he done himself in a motor. Seems more sense in that than dying for the politicians in my book. There ain't nothing worth kicking off for, it seems to me, than me and mine. Flags is for them that can afford the poles to hang 'em on. There's others who'd have it different, but that's their look-out. Me, I'll stay out of their uniform just so long as I can keep walking away. Anyway, they're a bit fussy about old lags, rather have young fellows with clean sheets and their mother's milk on their lips.'

He drew out a lighter and made a flame to dangle the IOU in. It caught and burned in one bright burst.

'We all bury our own,' he said, 'and in our own way.'

'Yes,' I said.

He dropped the last crisping piece into the sand with the cigar butt and the cigarette ash. He had forgotten about me.

I got out as fast as I could without making a noise. My watch said it was ten minutes to opening and I hurried down to the nearest pub. I felt like I'd just caught a disease that made my neck permanently dirty.

Thirteen

The saloon bar of the Cherry Tree was as empty as the upturned spirit bottles in the optics. I ordered a pint, looking through the carved glass into the other bar. A young bloke with a nervous look was counting the price of a half of mild onto the counter with his face half turned away. He was dying to look through at me but didn't have the courage. It was a long time since I had seen him last. He took his glass over to one of the tables and sat in a chair next to somebody reading a *Daily Mirror*.

The newspaper dropped down and Ernie looked over the top of it at me. His stout had lost its head from waiting. He picked it up, took an inch off the top and went out, folding the newspaper. I gave him a couple of minutes to get down the road, put the money the colonel had given me into an envelope with Manny's name and address on it and sealed it. The stamp was already on. I dropped it into my pocket and sank my pint in one. The young bloke watched me go, gulping at his drink, his adam's apple bobbing.

I walked slowly down to Hampstead Underground station in the light dusk. There wasn't much traffic and few pedestrians. I dropped the envelope into the box on the corner and went over the crossing, feeling for small coins for the automatic machines. A shilling got me a ticket to Whitechapel and change. The lift doors were just closing as I went down the emergency stairs. Ernie was leaning against the wall around the first bend.

'Still got him?' he said.

'Right behind.'

We went down a couple more spirals and stopped and waited. It wasn't long before we heard him coming—fast, and making a lot of noise in his hurry. He turned the corner above us and fell into my arms. I got him in a double arm lock and shoved his face up against the tiles. His head scraped across them, leaving a white trail.

'What d'you ... what are you doing?' he yelled.

Ernie put a hand over his mouth and flicked his razor open in the other, holding it close to the bloke's face.

'You,' said Ernie.

'Now,' I said, 'when I tell my mate to take his hand off your mouth, you're gonna do one of two things. You're gonna spill what we want or you're gonna shout the odds. If you do that you'll get carved. You'll have just enough time to think what a daft bleeder you've been before you go out. You got that?'

He nodded behind Ernie's palm.

'That's good,' I said. 'So far at least. Now, you've been dogging me. Been at it for a good long stretch. Invasion of privacy is that. You ain't doing it off your own back, that's obvious. Now, what we want is easy. Just who put you on me, names I can recognise, and why. Understand, nebish?'

He nodded again. Ernie's razor flashed in a sharp arc and the bloke's tie fell away from the knot.

'Sharp, ain't it?' said Ernie, moving his hand.

'What's your game, Sunshine?' I said.

'Look, they just said "see where he goes", that's all.'

'Who said?'

'They did. Just keep notes. Times and stuff. You know.'

'Who, you thick bastard?' I said, and gave his arm another twist. He sucked in his breath and kept his eyes on the razor. His voice fluttered like a budgie's wings.

'I told them I only did divorces. They wouldn't listen.'

'Who wouldn't?'

'I'm telling you.'

'Have his pockets out,' I said. Ernie patted him all over, found a wallet and passed it to me. I let go of the bloke's arms and let Ernie take care of him. There was an identity card with *James Allison* written inside. He lived at an address off Camden Town. There were half a dozen dog-eared business cards, all with different names and firms on. Only one tallied with the identity card. It said: *DISCREET ENQUIRIES*, and underneath, *Presented by James Allison (Director)*. Nothing else meant much, except a diary in his top pocket with dates and times pencilled in.

'Well, Jimmy Allison,' I said with a handful of his collar. 'A private nosey, eh?'

'A what?' said Ernie.

'Divorce enquiries,' said Allison. 'I told you that. I told them, but they wouldn't listen.'

I watched his face change colour as I gave him a short left, low down. He folded over slowly with his arms crossed over his stomach, one foot slipping onto a lower step.

'Who, Jimmy?' I said into his ear. 'Who'd you tell?'

Noises came out of his open mouth as he slid down inside his jacket. Just noises, no words.

'Come on, bubble up,' said Ernie.

'I don't ... know,' Allison gasped. 'Don't.'

'Let me give his mother a sewing job,' snarled Ernie. I let go of Allison's collar and let him flop all the way down onto his backside.

'He'll tell us,' I said.

Allison craned up at me with very white eyes, his head moving from side to side.

'Can't, want to, but can't. I don't honestly know. Please, they didn't tell me names. They came. Oh, God.' He stopped talking and cuddled himself harder. 'You've hurt me, I mean really.'

'Not so much as we will,' said Ernie. 'Come on, Bergie,

let's give him a stroking he won't live down.'

'You heard him, Jimmy,' I said. 'What's it to be?'

'Look,' Allison said, 'I don't know any names. I owed a bookie some money, a lot of money I couldn't pay. These two came to my place and said I could forget it if I did a job for them.' He looked up at me with creased eyes. 'Following you. Just to follow you. They told me when you were coming out of Pentonville and I followed you. That's all. They didn't tell me why. They just said to do it.'

'Who was the bookie?'

'What's the difference?'

'Just tell me.'

'Hyman. But it wasn't him. These fellows said they'd paid it up and I owed them. I've never seen them since. They just phone when they want to know something. They gave me a number to call once. I checked it out and it was a public booth by the docks.'

'So how long have you been on my arse?'

'A few days, straight. I lost you after that first day in King's Cross. They didn't like that much, but what could I do? Then I saw you at one of the addresses they told me to watch. They had a list of about forty. I told them I couldn't watch all of them. But they said it didn't matter. It didn't matter a bit.'

'What you reckon?' asked Ernie.

'It sounds straight,' I said.

'What's in it for me to lie?' gasped Allison. 'I'm hurt.'

'Where's the list?'

'List?'

'The list of addresses.'

'Taped to the back of a picture in my place. I didn't want to carry it on me. In case.'

'In case this happened.'

'Something like.'

'What a bloody cream-puff,' said Ernie. 'I've seen more backbone in a piece of rock salmon.'

'When did you talk to these two faces last?'

Allison didn't answer. He just lost all the blood in his face.

'That means recent,' said Ernie. He took hold of Allison's shirt collar and used the razor on the buttons. They clicked onto the iron steps.

'Don't . . .' moaned Allison.

'When?'

'I don't know. Last week, maybe.'

'Try again.'

'They'll . . . they'll . . .'

'It's them or us, son. Take your choice.'

'Yesterday morning.'

'After my run out to Hammersmith.'

'That's it.'

'So they know where I doss out?'

'No.'

'What d'you mean no.'

'I lost you at Whitechapel Station. I got to the top of the stairs and you'd gone.'

'That figure, Bergie?'

I said it did. Allison cuddled himself and looked at us in turn. A train growled into the station below shaking the stairs with vibration. A guard yelled something and footsteps began rattling in the passages. There was a hiss and bang as the doors closed, then the rising whine of the train running off into the tunnel.

'Last question, Jimmy boy,' I said to Allison, bending over him. 'What did these faces look like, how'd they dress?'

'They were big, both of them. Wide, you know?'

'Yes.'

'The one that did most of the talking was tall too, and blond. Nice suits, too. Good cut and always a different one. He always had a handkerchief here, in his top pocket. Snappy dresser.'

'Smile a lot, did he?'

'All the time. But he wasn't laughing.'

'That fits,' I said.

'Got to be,' said Ernie. 'Got to.'

'Now, Jimmy. The other one.'

'Shorter and squat. Dark chin and black hair. He didn't ever have much to say ever. Irish, I think he was. I'm not good at accents.'

'Nor much else, either, seems to me. That enough, Bergie?' said Ernie.

'I reckon.'

We both stood over Allison in a tinny silence. He looked back with unsteady eyes, his hands kneading his ribs. Even the backs of his wrists were sweaty.

'Up,' I said to him.

'What are you going to do?'

Ernie heaved him upright, scraping him along the wall and leaving another clean patch.

'Up, he said.'

'And up I meant,' I said. 'Give us the shiv.'

Ernie slapped it into my palm.

'Please,' said Allison, 'please?'

I caught him by the shirt-front and slashed down across his stomach. He squealed through clenched teeth, little bubbles of froth on his lips.

'You ain't hurt,' I said and pushed him away from me. He stood with his eyes closed and his arms criss-crossed, his trousers around his ankles and the severed belt in a coil over his shoes. He was crying.

Ernie and I walked off down the stairs leaving the sobs behind us.

The southbound platform was empty except for four squaddies and a sergeant at the far end, passing a single cigarette from mouth to mouth.

'How's Dolly?' I asked.

'Having trouble getting her booze. Makes her even more touchy than any single woman's a right to be. That, and there being no real market for hot money, she takes a lot of putting up with.'

'It's bad all over.'

'Look, Bergie, what you reckon to taking off for a bit? Out to the provinces or something. It's getting to be no joke the way things are. There's nothing moving anywhere. They know you're collecting on them IOUs, it'd be sense to let that lie. Burn the rest. You've done the best of them as it is. Why sweat over a few bob when the candle's this short?'

'I dunno,' I said. 'There's something on. Why would Laurie get a clown like that Allison to trail me when it could be done by any of their own runners? Don't that strike you as a bit dodgy?'

'No.'

'You're wetter than I thought. Wake up, son. There's something more important than me for Spanner to bother with. I can see him leaving Laurie free to do for me his way, but Laurie's farmed me out to a bloody incompetent. Does that sound like sense?'

'I dunno.'

'That geezer with Laurie, the one young Jimmy described. Does he tally with anyone you know?'

'No. There never was no bog-wallopers in Spanner's mob. Never one.'

'Maybe there ain't now.'

'What's that mean?'

'Just maybe a contract off the ferry.'

'Someone from outside, you mean?' Ernie said, and snorted deep in his throat. 'This is the Smoke, for gawd's sake. Not bloody Chicago. It don't happen.'

'I don't know,' I said.

'It don't. When did you hear of anything like that, eh? When?'

'Never.'

'Well, then.'

As far as Ernie was concerned there was no question.

Black was black and white was opposite. It had never happened so it couldn't. There were rules and ways of doing things, it was that simple.

The soldiers had drifted up the platform and were in a loose ring around us, not talking. The single cigarette was in the sergeant's hand and as I looked at him he drew a last lungful of smoke from it and dropped it under his boot, crushing it with a circular movement.

'Want a word with you, lad,' he said over Ernie's head.

'Me?' I said.

The squaddies were taking off their belts and wrapping them around their knuckles, closing up the circle.

'That's right,' said the sergeant. He pulled his pay-stick out from under his arm and held it out like a teacher at a blackboard, the tip against my chest. 'You with him?' he said to Ernie.

'No,' I said.

'Yeah,' said Ernie, 'so what?'

'So what, little feller,' said the sergeant, 'means you'll get a good hiding along with your mate if you don't make yourself scarce. That's so what.'

'You what?'

'You heard him,' said a squaddy. 'Hop it.'

'Like buggery I will.'

Ernie's hand was down deep in his waistcoat pocket where he kept his razor. Up against the soldiers he looked like a midget. There was still nobody else on the station. Just a broom closet behind me and a row of fire buckets filled with sand and dog-ends.

'Why me?' I asked. 'I never saw any of you before.'

'Seen you, though,' said the sergeant, prodding with his stick. 'Seen you up at the colonel's house. Now you know.'

Now I knew.

'Still want some, half-pint?' said the squaddy, grinning down at Ernie. Ernie didn't answer. I leaned back against the wall with my elbow on the end bucket.

'Not me, mate,' I said. 'Got the wrong feller. Don't know any colonels. Nor any other kind of khaki-coloured clowns.'

'Cully,' said the sergeant. The squaddy leering down at Ernie said: 'It's him. No doubt.'

'Right.'

The pay stick went up and back and started down again. I got hold of the bucket handle and heaved it in a circle. It caught the sergeant in the ribs, high under the armpit. He went forward and past me, the stick pinging off the wall and rolling off the platform onto the lines. I let the bucket go and ducked under a swinging belt buckle.

The squaddy the sergeant called Cully was holding up a red arm with blood spurting from between his fingers. Ernie swung again and Cully's battledress opened across the front, showing his cut shirt and a red line across his chest. He went down squealing.

A buckle hit me in the face. I got my hands on another bucket, got it up into my shoulder and threw it. Somebody grunted and fell away. A boot caught me in the ribs, another in the small of the back. I could hardly breathe. I was caught round the throat and around the waist with somebody kicking at my legs. We all went down in a heap, one under and one on top of me.

I used my knee on the one under me, catching him fair and square in the scrotum. His legs jack-knifed, pushing me and the other soldier off. We rolled almost to the edge of the platform with me underneath. His hands were around my throat with the belt across my windpipe. My lungs were empty and my arms were trapped under me. I sat up with everything I had, my chin tucked in. The top of my head caught him across the bridge of the nose and smashed it. He went quiet and heavy, falling across my lap.

I couldn't move him off my legs quick enough. I

caught sight of a boot swinging at me before a bomb-burst filled the inside of my chest with pain. I went back with my head over the edge of the platform, trying to breathe, trying to think, trying to see. All three hurt.

The ground vibrated under me as the rails began to hum. There was a train in the tunnel.

'Get Porter off his legs and get the bastard up,' said the sergeant.

The weight was suddenly gone and I was being lifted.

'Looks like he's out.'

'That ain't stopping me.'

I rolled forward in the soldier's arms and let him take my weight.

'Hold him up,' said the sergeant.

'I can't. You do it.'

'Right.'

The sergeant grabbed a handful of my hair. As he jerked my head up I laced my fingers into a double fist and swung up hard. I hit the sergeant under the chin with a jar that numbed both my arms. He went down as though he'd never been taught to walk. The soldier behind me let go and stepped back and away. Then he was running for all he was worth, up the stairs to the exit, leaving echoes behind.

Cully was on his knees up against one of the seats, wrapping his hand in the remains of his shirt. The sergeant and the one with the broken nose were still and lying where they had fallen. Ernie was leaning against a chocolate machine under a poster for Startrite shoes. His chest heaved and his foot was planted on the other soldier. His eye was swollen and turning blue.

'You all right?'

'Yeah, Bergie. Handsome.'

I looked down at the squaddy he had his foot on.

'What's wrong with him?'

'I bust me shiv on the wall. Had to butt him in the cobs. He went down peaceful.'

The train thundered into the station and screamed to a halt. We waited for the people to get off, found an empty carriage and got in. The guard hustled down the platform to where Cully was sitting.

'What happened, soldier?'

'Manoeuvres,' said Cully. 'Practising realistic drill.'

'Get on,' said the guard. 'Looks real, that blood.'

'Get on yourself, dad. Or you'll be late at the end of the line.'

The guard got back into the train, closed the doors and we rolled off into the singing dark with the pipes and cables flashing past the windows.

Ernie nudged me, handing over a lighted Woodbine. 'I tell you,' he said, 'everybody's team-handed these days.'

I sucked on the cigarette and listened.

'But two's better than thousands if they know what's what,' he said in a cloud of smoke. 'That's what I reckon.'

'Just wake me when we're there,' I said, and closed my eyes.

Fourteen

The factories were turning out the late shifts as I walked down Middlesex Street, and men with the marks of their machine-minding on their faces surged around me like a soiled river. They walked in groups and lines, making tired jokes to each other about three-legged greyhounds and the studding abilities of racing pigeons.

There was a closeness about them that I found unsettling. All these blokes with their factory matiness, the clubs they had for darts and social outings, the wives they went home to every night, the kids they raised to think and do as they did. The rotten wages they worked for, and the crawling they had to do around the bosses to keep bringing in a few quid to pay off the tally-man, the rent and the Provident cheques.

Maybe enough left over on a Saturday night for a pint and a game of arrows with the lads. A lie-in on Sunday morning with a big head and then on with the stiff best boots and a collar and tie to sit in the front room with the relations around for high tea with whelks and maybe butter on the bread. All set out on the best china and no snatching or eating with your mouth open like the other days of the week; the kids up at the table instead of under it, stiff little dolls squirming inside the too-tight clothes and not daring to do more than nod when spoken to for fear of a belt round the head for talking out of turn. They might have been foreign for all I understood them.

There was a gap in the high brick walls with two upturned cannon set in the paving before it. I turned down it away from the press and let the alley lead me out to another road where rows of high flats looked out onto the back walls of the factories. The view didn't have any takers, all the windows were empty of faces. Just rows of streaky glass panes with net curtains in every one.

I turned into the street and walked along looking at the numbers, hard to see under caked soot and chalked slogans. Many were obscene and most illegible. Kids swarmed everywhere, yelling and wrestling and skipping in rows. I threaded through them and went into the door I wanted. There were dustbins lining the narrow hallway and the flies were big and glossy. A notice on the wall told me that the rubbish chutes were blocked due to misuse. The walls sweated with the stink.

I went up a couple of flights and rapped on the door with 6 chalked on it. A piece of lino was nailed over the letter box and the transom window was filled with cardboard. I watched a twenty-eight-stone granny huff down the stairs past me as I waited for the door to be answered. She smelled like a dead horse.

The piece of lino lifted and a pair of eyes looked out at me.

'Hello, smiler,' I said.

The eyes disappeared and a child's voice yelled from behind the door: 'Mum. It's a man.'

'Who is he?' said a woman, with all the tiredness and resignation in the world.

'Dunno.'

Slippers shuffled up to the door and it opened about a thousandth of an inch.

'Whadja want?'

I smiled into the crack.

'Remember me?' I said.

There was a hesitation, then the woman said: 'Not me, I don't.'

'Friend of Ronny's. I was here once before. Good time ago now. I think you was carrying that one. The one that looked through the door. How old is she?'

'She's an 'im,' said the woman.

'Nice little feller.'

'He's a bastard. What's on? I don't know you as a friend of my Ron's. Anyhow, he's gone.'

'I know, lady. That's why I'm here.'

'What you want?' she asked again. I could feel her thinking over her shoulder at a sink full of washing up and the ironing that she ought to be getting round to.

'I ain't selling and I ain't collecting. If you like, I'll shout it out from here so the whole street knows.'

The door swung inwards to show me a thin-faced girl in a faded cardigan and flower print dress. She had a pair of men's slippers on her feet and a pair of ankle socks. She was as grey as her voice.

'You'd better come in. The place is a mess, I can't seem...'

Her hand made a downward gesture as she shuffled away up the passage. I stepped inside and forced the door shut. The wallpaper had been around a long time but everything in the passage was clean. There was a good shine on the lino. She pushed open another door and waved into it.

'In here,' she said, and went through without waiting. I followed her. She sat in an uncut moquette chair and cuddled her knees, the child hanging on her shoulder, staring at me under a tangled fringe. I sat in a matching chair facing her.

She had once been pretty. Maybe still was, but it was hard to tell under her dead eyes. It was impossible to hold her gaze. She was a ghost trapped in a permanent funeral cortège.

I gave her a cigarette and she held it between her knitted fingers, ignoring the lighter I held out. I lit up my own and put the lighter in my pocket.

'You was here once,' she said. 'Only, Ron...'

'I came here with him the once. You hadn't been

married long. We did some business together. Said he was buying you a coat with his end.'

'The coat. Yes.'

'You remember?'

'It was a lovely one,' she said to the air. 'A full-length with a fur collar and edging round the sleeves. Buttons with real leather and gold round the outside. As black as black.'

She rewore it inside her head with the vaguest curve at the corners of her mouth as she smoothed the front of herself with her hands. The cigarette sticking out between her fingers like a piece of white bone. The boy didn't seem to notice that his mother was elsewhere, he hung onto her, gnawing his fist and staring at me in the direct rude way only children are capable of. I stared back and neither of us blinked. The girl lost her dream and was sitting in the chair again, looking down at the cigarette as if it had grown there. She tapped it on a knuckle and put it carefully between her lips in the way infrequent smokers do. I lit it for her and she pecked at it with tight lips in little puffs.

'Man bleeding,' said the boy.

She looked down at my hands, taking in the wide knife-scar on the back of the left one and the skinned knuckles on both of them. Her eyes came up to mine to look at me out of their dark lost depths. They held me for a long moment before they ran down to my hands and stayed there.

'Your name's Berg-something,' she said. 'My Ron used to say about a mate called that. You was always coming up. He said ...'

She pursed her lips and frowned at something that hovered between us, a phrase or an image. All I could see were the writhing plumes of smoke. Her teeth came together in a hard little click as though she was biting on it to keep it in focus.

'He said you were a good ... mate. One of the best.'

'He was a bit special to me,' I said.

'Bergie,' she said, 'that's right. Bergie's one of the best. A good mate.' Her words came out separately as though she were eight years old and reading them from a primer. The room was stuffy. Filled with things of yesterday, fragments of a man that had lived there once, and would never leave so long as she could remember him. It had been a mistake to come into this private chapel.

'Look, girl,' I said, 'I did a bit of business with Ronny before he . . .'

'It was a road accident,' she broke in. It was as if I hadn't spoken. 'A taxi outside his work. They said he didn't feel any pain. It was quick. The doctor told me that. Instantaneous, he said. That's a long word for something that was so . . . quick.'

'Yes.'

'He was good to the boy.'

'Yes.'

'Oh, yes. Always.'

I tried again.

'I didn't see Ronny before it happened. I was holding some money. His money. He earned it. All square and legal.'

'First he was there and then he wasn't. I want him back all the time. All the time. Sometimes, I hear someone run up the stairs like he did. Or whistle in the street. And, and I run to the door. It's always somebody else. Or there's no one there at all. It happens all the time. All the time.'

She was off where nobody could reach her. Higher than where the cigarette smoke curled against the ceiling, higher maybe than the roof three storeys above that. I couldn't follow her and I didn't want to. I pressed my dog-end against the side of the grate in the fireplace and got up. She didn't notice. The boy watched me take the envelope out of my inside pocket and lean it against a picture on the mantelpiece. It was a framed snap of

Ronny in shirtsleeves with his arm around the pretty girl that the woman in the chair used to be.

'Tell your mum that's for her,' I told the boy. 'You tell her, right?'

He nodded at me like a small pink owl.

'I tell.'

I patted his tangled head and went out into the passage. When I looked back he had climbed into his mother's lap and was snuggled up against her, his fist in his mouth. She had her arm around him just to stop him falling onto the floor. The cigarette curled smoke from the middle of her mouth as she looked intently at nothing. I went out onto the stinking stairs and closed the door of number 6 behind me. I breathed in with relief. A smell you can get used to.

Fifteen

The four o'clock hooter was about to go as I got to the gates of the Golden Sun Laundry. Through the top floor windows I could see blokes shrugging into their coats with one eye on the clock and the other on the door. Women crowded in the passage by the front entrance nattering at each other.

The uniformed bloke at the main gate looked down at the note I held out without taking it. He squinted up at me as if I was a fifth columnist with a bomb in each boot and a swastika embroidered on my underpants. He was little and old and suspicious.

'You Roberts?' I said.

He pulled a watch from his waistcoat pocket as far as the Albert would stretch and watched it tick up to the hour. The hooter went and he grunted to himself.

'Who's asking?' he said.

I stuffed the note into his hand.

'Read that and you'll know as much as I do.'

He unfolded the square of paper and read the cramped freehand with his lips moving. He wasn't pleased with what the note told him. The workers came out in a rush, elbowing through the gates to the pavement and the bus stops. I watched over the bobbing heads and goodnights as Roberts read the note through a second time. He found my face over the crush and made a wry face.

'This straight up?' he yelled.

I nodded.

''Night, Robbo,' called a fat woman in a waterproof

pixie hat. 'Watch out for parachuters.' She giggled off with her arms linked with two other laughing women. Roberts gave me another sour look and said:

'If they came in as fast as they get out of it, we might get on with winning the bleeding war.'

I lit up and looked bored. The crowd began to thin out a bit. A few people said goodnight to Roberts; most of them didn't. He read the note again; at least, he stared at it for a bit.

'This says Albert can't relieve me. That right, he's laid up and you're his nephew?'

'Yeah. Poor old monkey's got a touch of the old trouble. Pitiful it is, the way he's lying there. White as his pillow and moaning,' I said, shaking my head. 'I hate to see it.'

The last time I'd seen Albert he'd been upright in his armchair with ropes holding him still and his mouth full of handkerchief, his face more purple than white. It had taken a long time to get him to write the note.

'The uniform won't go anywhere near. You're too big,' said Roberts.

'Uniform? Not this kiddy. Gawd blimey, I only offered to sit it out here tonight as a favour. Not to let you down, like. Nothing was said about no bloody uniform. Still, if you want to handle a double stretch that's your business. Me, I was just trying to help out.'

I let him think about it. He looked at the note, at his watch, back at the note and over at the laundry. It was a toss-up between hanging about an empty building all night or his feet up in front of the fire with a fish supper out of a newspaper.

'I dunno,' he said, 'it ain't strictly up to me. That's the personnel manager's job, ain't it? He's the one to decide.'

'Up to you. But make your mind up. I'm the one doing the old feller a favour. No skin off mine what you do.'

'Yeah, but he's not here, is he?'

'Who ain't?'

'That personnel manager. Left early for the weekend. Shouldn't have, but he did.'

I shrugged and flicked my cigarette into the gutter.

'That's it, then. Well, I'll tell the old feller it wasn't on. Course, he'll fret himself a bit. Can't be helped. Teddah.'

'Hang on,' said Roberts. 'I won't get off till dinner time tomorrow when the Sunday bloke comes on. And he's only coming in to open up for the maintenance crew. Not that they'll do much neither. Play cards mostly, and keep the boilers going for the Monday shift. Money for old rope.'

'Some have it real soapy. Me, I'm on a fifty-twoer waiting for a posting. Probably get shoved out to some dead and alive hole guarding some capitalist's sheep in the Midlands. Makes you weep.'

'In the cake, eh?' said Roberts with a sharp smile. 'I was in the first lot. Wouldn't have me for this one. Past it.'

'There's more than a handful they've said that to.'

The last worker went out through the gate wheeling a bike. He jumped into the saddle and cycled past the bus queue. Roberts slid the wire gates almost closed and beckoned me through the gap. I stepped through as he fixed the padlocks and chains.

'It's a doddle,' he said. 'All you do is check all the doors every hour and keep your ears open for anybody wandering about outside. It's kids mostly. Get over the wire and break the windows. Buggers round here they are. Steal anything that's not bolted down, burn anything that is. Do it for devilment.'

'We all have in our time,' I said.

He showed me over the place in double-quick time. It was an L-shaped building on three floors with a basement filled with boilers, pipes and steam. There's nothing so throat-clogging as the smell of stale steam. The ironers and pressers were on the ground floor, along with the boilers for the wet wash. Invisible mending was on the first floor and the top floor was given over to offices.

He showed me his little cubby-hole down in the basement where he and Albert brewed up, told me how to handle the gas ring, then showed me how to let him out of the back of the building through a blind door. Then he gave me the keys and was off down the alley without a backward glance. I waved anyway. He didn't even pause at the corner, there was a brief gleam of light from his shiny peak and he was gone. I waited a good ten minutes to make sure, then went over to the dustbins in a row the other side of the alley, heaving the front three to one side. There were two sacks under a bit of tarpaulin where I'd stowed them the night before. I grabbed them by the necks and dragged them through the back door into the laundry. The door closed and locked itself.

I dropped the sacks into an empty linen bin and wheeled it out into the main room where the wicker laundry bins stood in rows with narrow aisles between them. The whole place smelled of heat and damp and bleach, of soap and cleaning fluid. The walls ran with wetness and the concrete was hot and dry under my shoes. How those women stood it for an eight-hour shift I couldn't understand. An egg would have fried on the slatted benches.

I pulled at the slip-knots at the necks of the sacks and they opened, spilling firelighters. As I passed each wicker basket I dropped a couple in. The names of the hotels and clubs they belonged to were stencilled on the sides. *The Starlight, Clphm.* had four baskets heaped with tablecloths, napkins and waiters' jackets. The stuff for the downstairs restaurant; upstairs was where the wheels turned, the chips went down onto numbered squares and the money was really made. Eight lighters for that money-spinner.

Next was a single basket marked *Rainbow, Plackett*

St. That's where the King Lears with the ready hung out, pulling in the young kids with bent arses and arms ready for the first needle. A plain front door that opened to members' keys and up one flight. One basket, six lighters.

A group of straight lahdie West End hotels next. All straight and no connections. One in each. Then four baskets painted orange, the stencilling in gold. *The Square Ring.* Spanner's own. His purple palace where he entertained and got photographed with his arm round the shoulders of the stars of stage, screen and radio. A baker's dozen for each.

The line finished with six baskets marked *Colfax Palace, Kens.* There wasn't a five-string pimp worth his ninety per cent who hadn't oiled his palm there with an exhibition or a gang-bang for the stone rich. Not to mention the candid photos on the side to be delivered to milady if money didn't pass across at regular intervals. I scooped a couple of handfuls of Zips into each. Funny that even in a laundry all the villains managed to get together.

It didn't take much to finish off. I tied a couple of dozen bedsheets together and draped them from basket to basket, running the last few yards along the passage to the back door. There were cans of cleaning fluid in a store with a lock that a kid could have opened with the sharp end of a cornet. I opened all the taps and let the stuff run out. One can I took and poured fluid all along the knotted sheets. An Irish linen fuse. I stood a candle at the end of the sheets with a foot of jelly fuse set in the wax an inch down from the top. When the candle burned down it would light the fuse, spark down to the sheets and off and running.

I left the candle unlit and went down to the watchmen's cubby-hole in the basement and used the phone. Manny answered before the first double buzz was finished.

'Can you talk?' I asked.

'Talk I can, and talk I will,' he said in a thick voice. 'So now where are you? No, don't tell me, my old pump couldn't take it. Wait for a call you said this morning. Just wait. So what does Manny do? He waits, that's what he does. He waits through breakfast. He waits through dinner and half-way through tea. Did you say wait until this evening? No. Am I made of iron for all this waiting?'

He would have gone on but I broke in.

'Manny, you sound like an old mum wittering over her twelve-year-old daughter. Listen, get Ernie to bring the jam-jar round, will you? I could use a lift.'

'Round? Round to where?'

'The Golden Laundry. Round back. I'll be waiting.'

'I don't want to ask. I don't, but I have to. What are you doing in Mister Spandrell's place of legitimate business, may I ask? Stealing underwear maybe?'

'It's a cool night. I thought I'd warm it up. Tell Ernie, will you? Oh, and after your tea you can sort out the divi-up on the collection money. I'll be round tomorrow night for my end. Teddah.'

I went back up the stairs and lit the candle to test for draughts. The flame grew straight and tall without a flicker. I pinched it out and went to look out of the window. The balloons were up and the street beyond the locked wire gates was free of traffic and the forecourt was empty. I couldn't get used to how quiet London had got since petrol rationing. You hardly saw a private car. Just buses, the odd cab and a few lorries, mostly military. My watch told me it was just after five when the sirens started all round the building.

A black saloon went along the street, slowed at the gates, then accelerated away out of sight. I reached for my cigarettes and put them away again. The place was filled with fumes. The saloon went past again, slower, in the opposite direction, faces at all the windows. Its wheels turned into the kerb and it coasted to a stop behind the boundary wall of the building next door, just as the alert wound down and faded away. It was time to go, car or no car.

The view from the rear window was as crisp as noon but the alley was too narrow to see far in either direction. No Ernie. No car. No voices and nothing moving. Just bins and shadows.

I crossed back to the front of the building and watched men dropping off the wire fence onto the tarmac with hardly a rattle. Another jumped from the pavement to catch at the chain-link fence and start to climb.

A small man in uniform and a hat with a shiny peak stood behind them looking at the main doors. Shrewd little Roberts. Another man, in shirtsleeves, joined him. It was Albert without his handkerchief and ropes. I should have reckoned on Roberts looking his mate up to see how he was.

I went to the back door and listened until my ears sang. Nothing. I lit the candle and was out in the alley without a sound. Two men were coming down towards me from the right. They didn't stop or look surprised when they saw me, they just came on without hurry. There were two more coming from the other direction. There was nowhere to run.

An engine roared and tyres squealed on the cobbles.

I looked to the right again and there behind the men was my car with Ernie under his cap at the wheel. They looked over their shoulders, stopped, and then started running at me. The two on my left stood still. Ernie bore down on them, his foot all the way down, the roar of the engine racketing off the walls. Just as the bonnet nudged at the running men they dived to either side of the alley, going down in a clatter of bins and boxes. The car halted beside me with the door gaping, Ernie grinning through it.

'Move it up!' he yelled.

I dropped in beside him and the car leapt away in

pursuit of the other two as they ran with their arms pumping, heads half-turned towards us. They reached the end of the alley a fraction ahead of us and threw themselves aside.

Ernie twisted the wheel and slammed on the brake. The car slid sideways, drifting out of the alley. The off-side rear mudguard caught a pile of boxes at the corner, throwing them across the road. One sailed over the car and burst on the bonnet. Paper and card made a brief snowstorm; then we were through it and making for the main road.

'Make a right,' I said. 'They're all over the front of the building.'

Ernie ignored me, pulling the wheel in the opposite direction; accelerating out of the turn past the laundry and towards the parked saloon. Three men were scrambling up the wire and another was crossing the pavement pulling something from under his overcoat. He ran straight out in front of us, the barrel of his shotgun coming up. It was level with his eyes when we hit him.

There was a sound like a paper bag bursting as he banged against the windscreen and rolled away onto the road, the shotgun going off with a double roar.

'I told you right,' I yelled, 'bloody right.'

Ernie shook sweat from his forehead in a sheet.

'Nothing doing, cocker,' he yelled back. 'That geezer would have let us have it up the khyber.'

I was slammed back in my seat as we went into a snaking skid. Something blurred across us as we weaved, something with tyres higher than our bonnet and tarpaulin sides that cut out the sky. We braked and I lost focus as my head went forward against the dash. I put my hands up to my face as Ernie crashed through the gears. He found reverse and my elbows were pressed down into my lap as the car jumped backwards—backwards and away from the lorry as it ran up the kerb and into the bus shelter. One wall of the shelter tore up into separate slats and the roof dropped onto the lorry's bonnet; the metal sign pecking down through the top of the cab. Steam billowed everywhere.

We turned in our own length as Ernie braked and turned the wheel, slewed onto the pavement between the wall and a street lamp and bounced back into the road, gathering speed. Ahead of us a lot of things were all happening at once.

The bloke with the shotgun had ejected the used cartridges and was rummaging through his pockets for two more. He could hardly hold the gun still for shaking.

The three men were still on the wire fence, one straddling the top as the others climbed. There was too much movement in the wire for him to get his other leg across.

Roberts' shiny cap lay on the pavement with a broken brim as he and Albert ran as distant figures down the road.

The black saloon had turned and was racing towards us with Poncer at the wheel, his face as black as the paintwork and too many teeth in his mouth. Ernie drove straight at him, swearing in a monotone without repeating himself. I braced myself for the crash.

We were about a bonnet's length apart when Ernie swerved across the road, running up the pavement on the laundry side, the saloon only half a length behind and closing fast. The men on the wire watched us coming, their faces as frozen as their limbs, just hanging there. Then we hit the gates and were under and past them.

The iron gate-stanchions squealed out of the ground as our bonnet nosed into the wire like a blue fish in a metal net. The air was filled with whipping coils and we were losing speed as the fence dragged at the car, engine racing and the tyres spinning.

I was reaching for the handle and yelling to Ernie to get out when the saloon rammed us. We reared up as the rest of the fence sprang apart, all the windows opaquing. We leapt forward across the forecourt with the saloon locked on behind. I drew back my fist and smashed it through the windscreen in time to see the main doors come up at us and burst apart as we hurtled inside the laundry. There was a sensation of motion and impact before silence and numbness took over.

Sixteen

I opened my eyes. It couldn't have been much later, but I felt warm and rested. The ground floor stretched away from me with the wicker bins on the ceiling and the sprinkler valves and pipes on the floor. I kicked out and got myself out of the car. The seat fell out beside me and glass tinkled. The door and mudguard were somewhere else. I rolled onto my stomach and set the world upright. A pair of feet stuck out from beyond what had been the bonnet of my car, only one had a shoe on. They were Ernie's socks.

I called his name. He didn't answer or grunt or scream. His toes didn't even twitch. I had to go and look at him and I didn't want to. I just wanted to lay where I was and not do anything. Anything at all.

'Can you see anything?' said Poncer.

'Not a bastard thing,' somebody answered.

Engines droned in the sky far off to the East and big guns coughed. Poncer swore.

'Well you won't from there,' he said. 'Have a clock over the top of the car.'

Feet scraped as somebody got to his feet. I crawled round to Ernie and looked at him. He lay on his back with his chest going up and down and his eyes closed. There wasn't a mark on him.

Petrol was running out of the tank into a puddle from the radiator, making rainbow patterns on the concrete.

'Well?' said Poncer.

'Nothing. I told you. The bloody place stinks of petrol. Tank must have gone. One spark in there, and wallop.'

'That's all we bloody well need. Gimme that shooter and get on down to that window. Have it in when I say. I'm going in here. Right?'

'Right.'

I got my arms under Ernie's back and pulled him up and over my shoulder. He weighed no more than an overcoat. I stood up, hefted him and ran off down the stairs into the basement. Poncer made a noise in his throat and there was a double roar. A laundry bin at the end of the aisle kicked up and ran off on its castors with bits of wicker spraying out. Shot spat and sang through the pipes.

I stumbled into the watchmen's cubby-hole and dropped Ernie into a chair. It was like he was made of string. I had to drape him over the table to stop him rolling on to the floor. His mouth had dropped open and I could see where he needed fillings. He didn't look very pretty, his colour was bad.

I dialled the three nines for Emergency and half heard the burrs at the exchange as I listened to Poncer grunting over the car roof. Glass smashed beyond him and pieces skittered down the stairs.

'Emergency,' said a woman's voice.

'Fire,' I whispered. 'There's a fire.'

She said something I couldn't catch. Poncer had edged to the top of the stairs. The double barrel of his shotgun showed beyond the wall.

'Look, lady—there's a fire at the Golden Laundry. Tell 'em to step on it,' I said, and rang off. The bell sounded like Quasimodo doing his pieces when I put the receiver down.

'Nothing here, Ponce,' a man called.

'Yeah, nothing,' grunted another as he climbed through the door frame. I could see their shadows crisp on the heavy lino of the passage.

Poncer stepped carefully into the passage with the shotgun poked forward and cuddled in against his waist.

He was grinning down at the wet prints that I'd trailed to the office doors. Without looking round he waved his free hand.

'Don't fret. I've got him,' he said.

I let him take another couple of steps before I called out, 'That's far enough, Poncer.'

He laughed, hefted the gun, and laughed again.

'You've pulled your last pudden, Bergman. You're potless and out of time.'

The shadows of the other two ran along the lino until they disappeared into the stair-well. There was a clatter of feet and there were two men peering over Poncer's shoulder. One had a torn trouser leg. They were both armed.

'Look around. Can you smell the fumes?' I called. 'Take a good look.'

'At what?' yelled Poncer without moving anything.

'There's a dozen drums of fluid on those floors. About a hundred gallons worth. One match in the right place and you'll be a memory.'

'He's right, Ponce.'

'Bluff. This bloke's full of it.'

'No Ponce, straight. Take a whiff.'

'Nothing. These places always smell this way.'

'Listen to them, Poncer,' I said. 'You can't even take a chance on pulling that trigger. One spark from a ricochet and that's it.'

'Bluff, you bluffing bastard,' he called back. 'All bluff.'

'It ain't,' said one of the blokes, 'look at them bins. Soaked in it...'

The rest of what he said was lost in a roar as Poncer fired the first barrel. The cubby-hole door lost its glass and banged wide open. The calendars and ARP posters on the wall dusted into confetti. Bits of plaster showered over Ernie and some of it went into his mouth. He didn't even blink.

I wanted to wipe his face but there wasn't time. I got

him up on my shoulder and fumbled my gun out. I had trouble getting the safety off one-handed. The door had swung closed and I waited for Poncer to kick it open again.

Poncer barged in, using his shoulder, the shotgun high up on his chest. He saw me and swung the gun round and down. I pointed at him and pulled the trigger. The explosion was deafening in the confined space. Poncer banged back against the wall as though he were on wires.

'Bluff,' he said, with his mouth open as wide as it would go. Very slowly his hands brought the gun up at me, up through a river of glue. I fired again. His shirt-front jumped and he was slumping and hooked over the glazing-bar of the door. His gun hung off the end of his arms, pointing out along the passage.

'You . . .' he said, then his mouth hung open as wet as a newly painted bus. Something went out of his face, leaving it without expression. His eyes looked at somewhere far off. Then his lids came down and he wasn't looking at anything. He was just a dead man hanging on a door.

It went very quiet, almost silent. But there were other sounds in the silence. Deep drones from engines high over the roofs. And high whistlings. Something crumped outside. There was a flash and a roar. All the air in the room was eaten in one hot breath. I was dumped in the corner with Ernie over and across me. Everything was hot and orange and the sound was too loud to hear. The room whited out as the ceiling came down. Stuff was falling down all around me. I got up and was knocked down again. The walls shook and the floor heaved.

I got up again. The desk had turned into a heap of broken wood and torn paper. Poncer and the door had parted company. I couldn't see him. The telephone had disappeared. There was just a frayed cord hanging out of the wall. Water was everywhere from the ruptured pipes. The passage to the head of the stairs was a tunnel of criss-crossing water jets. Bits of twisted metal were tumbled about the place, hissing and throwing off steam. The flames were a solid wall in the body of the laundry but the stairs were free. There was a chassis and a wheel where my car had been. I went up the stairs one at a time and out into the air.

The black saloon was on its side and one of its tyres was alight. The two men who had followed Poncer were crumpled heaps just past it, lying still with their clothes smouldering. There was a hole in the tarmac you could have dropped a bus into. A fractured water pipe stuck out of the bottom, geysering away. Everything was wet and edged with red from the fires. The factory next door had lost half a wall and most of its roof. Machinery showed through the holes.

There was a body tangled up in the perimeter wire and another on the pavement. They were still too. I went past without looking.

I went along the road under Ernie's weight. He felt like a pair of overweight twins. The pavement was twisting and looping ahead of me. It wouldn't stay still or continue to go in the same direction. It slid from side to side, grew hills and valleys that were sometimes soft underfoot; more often hard. A wall banged into me and I leaned against it. I went to put my gun away but it had gone. My fingers were made of boiled beetroot and they wouldn't keep still. Everything was the wrong colour.

I rolled Ernie to the ground and got him leaned up against the wall so that I could light a cigarette. I felt around but there weren't any where my pocket had been. I tried working that out but it couldn't be done. The things I wanted to think about were somewhere else.

Then there was a red fire engine at the kerb with men in helmets jumping off, unrolling cables. White snakes with red edges. Sound came and went in waves. One moment there were men shouting and bells ringing, then there weren't. Fire crackled, then it didn't. Everything smelled of burning.

An ambulance was there and stretchers with red blankets. Two men leaned over Ernie and a nurse made faces at me. I wished for a cigarette and they gave me one. It bobbed about in my mouth where they put it. Bobbed and jiggled all on its own. It didn't taste of anything.

The sound came back and they said the one on the ground was a goner and did I know him. I didn't know if I did or not. I knew Ernie but he wasn't dead. Ernie was somewhere else so I went to look for him. They wanted me to go in the ambulance with the dead man. But I didn't get in. I went away from them to look for Ernie. The road was straighter now. I could find him.

Seventeen

I found myself looking at the man on the cross with the praying women kneeling beneath him. They were all looking up at a golden cloud with calm painted faces. I had been looking at them for a long time. I don't think my face had any expression.

Every now and then, the stained-glass colours grew brighter as the fires outside were roused by the breeze. People around me were talking in the hushed voices everyone uses in a church. Even the hurt ones wailed quietly as they cuddled their burns. A woman with a dead baby sat in the next pew. She was quiet and didn't move. Nobody took it away from her. There was nowhere to put it and there were other things to do. Men coughed with nowhere to spit.

I had a blanket around me and a white mug in my hands. It had tea in it. I knew without sipping it it was cold. I'd been holding it a long time. At least the shaking had stopped. But there was still somebody I had to find. I couldn't remember who he was but he was nothing like the people in the window. I sipped the tea. It was cold.

'How you feeling, mate?' asked a warden. He had an old face under the soot. His eyes were very white and his tin hat had a dent in it. His overalls were more white than blue.

'You look better than when we found you,' he said. He rolled a cigarette with steady fingers. He didn't lose a shred of the tobacco. He licked the gummed edge and put it in my mouth. I let him light it for me and sucked hard. I took the smoke right down into my lungs and held it there.

'You was hanging on a wall and yelling somebody's name. You give us a bit of a dance getting you here.'

I let the smoke out in a jerk.

'Ernie, you was saying, Ernie. At the top of your voice. There was nobody with you. Mate of yours, this Ernie?'

'A mate.'

'It's a bit of a circus at the minute, but we'll help you look for him if you want. That's what we're here for.'

'Ernie's dead,' I found myself saying.

'Sorry.'

'Yeah.'

I looked back at the window. The green glass had been blown out. The two women were kneeling on a hole.

Pink streaked through the dawn sky. There were columns of smoke off towards the docks. Everything smelled of escaping gas and brick-dust. There was a mobile canteen at the end of my street where two women in tin hats served tea. They were doing brisk business with firemen and wardens. There was a hole where the greengrocer's had been. The back end of the baker's van stuck out from under his collapsed shop front. None of the houses had any windows with whole panes in them. You couldn't walk anywhere without crunching through glass.

I picked my way through the coiled hoses and rubble to my flat. The main door was off its hinges and lying half-way up the passage. There was glass all the way up the stairs. I let myself in and had to push hard to open the door. The ceiling had come down in the hall. The kitchen had lost its window and the light bulb was broken. The bedroom was untouched.

I washed with cold water from the tap; it came

through brown and smelling of chlorine. The face that looked back at me from the shaving mirror was a hundred years old. The forehead was bruised and raw, with a maze of tiny scratches under the right eye. A lot of skin was missing from the back of my hands and when I looked at them they started to hurt.

I changed my clothes right down to my socks, put on my best tie and sat on the bed. Then I let the tears come. There didn't seem to be any point to anything for a long time. Then I slept.

It was dark when I got to Manny's. I watched the street for a long time before I cut across to the boundary wall and went along to his place through the back gardens. I scratched on his window and his old-wise face peered out with the room empty behind him. He nodded at me without surprise and let me in. The moon was bright inside the room even without the light. I could see him as clear as day.

He lowered himself in a hard chair beside the kitchen table and poured tea into a glass. The usual lemon was missing. He stirred in half a spoonful of sugar and licked the spoon before dropping it onto the American cloth. His hands came together with the fingers twined, dropping into his lap like they belonged there. His eyes were shinier and wetter than I'd ever seen them.

'Drink your tea before it gets cold,' I said.

'So it'll get cold.'

His mouth hardly moved and his eyes stayed locked onto my face. He made me feel like I was in the bottom of a six-foot hole and he was waiting for the vicar to stop talking so that he could throw dirt down on me. I sat down so that I didn't have to think about my legs. All of me was cold but for my hands.

'There's worse things than cold tea,' said Manny. 'Like the dead under the rubble of a certain laundry.'

'I'll buy you a church if you wanna talk like that. You

think I knew it would have come out that way?'

'What you think now don't have a bearing. It's what Spanner thinks with that Poncer and five of his other boys topped that matters. Funny thing. He's cooler about it than I would have sussed. Had a long conversation, did me and Spanner. Very long.'

'He was here?'

'I was there. Sent some wheels with an invitation. Whatever you say about him, he don't let anything stop the flow of business.'

I let the silence gather as I thought about that.

'Yeah,' whispered Manny, 'thinking is something you got to be doing a lot of, the way things have sorted. Your name wasn't mentioned except in passing. No, we worked a little meat deal. We use Cliff's transport and I make the sale in the market. All I have to do is have one of my lads there to check out it's straight mutton, give me the word on the blower, and I call ahead to the warehouse. The sides get taken straight there and I don't even see it.'

'It smells,' I said. 'Why should he make you offers?'

Manny made a sound in his throat, unravelled his fingers and sipped his tea.

'You think this is the first time? Never. Must have worked most on twelve to a dozen like this with Spanner. You don't think he ignored me after that time with Poncer and you and Jacko bundling up and down my passage, do you? Think he'd write me off as if I had walls built round me? No, not him.'

'How come it was never mentioned before?'

'Why mention? Is it you pays my rent? Did we stand up and say I do forever and ever? Suddenly we're married yet?'

'We done some dealing for a few years, Manny. That counts a bundle with me. What's this all in aid of? I only came to get paid off from what I collected off the betting slips. I didn't come to get no final divorce. Why the big elbow? Why now, maybe nothing to do with your corns turning yellow, is it?'

'Maybe everything if that's how it cuts with you!'

Manny slapped his hands to his face and rocked his head back and forward behind them. When he lowered them, he said:

'Shouting I don't need. You I don't need. What I need is a peaceful life. Aggravation I've had in spades. By the bucketful. Now I got enough to do with bombs coming down and curdling the milk on my doorstep, without you shouting the odds all over the manor. It's time you was off to another town. Birmingham or Swansea. Somewhere with a fresh outlook where no one knows even the name of your tailor. What I'm saying is, it's time to stop all this Buck Ryan stuff. Get me?'

I moved my head up and down in slow jerks.

'Yeah, I get you, Manny. Like you was in the same room with me. The profits have started to look a bit thin from where you're sitting. What Laurie did to me don't count no more, nor that face in the taxi that spread Ronny all over King's Cross.'

'You're ahead. Six to two ain't such terrible odds.'

'You're behind, Manny. It's down to two to one. Ernie was with me last night. There's one more you can write off in your diary. Still, the way you're mouthing off, it looks like you still make a profit.'

'What...' Manny started.

'You've saved on a Christmas card.'

'Nobody said anything about Ernie, Bergie. As God is my judge.'

'Leave it out, will you? It's me that got him carved. You knew he was there. You called him up with the jam-jar for me. It was Goering or Poncer done him. What's the diff? He's done and gone.'

'It makes a difference. Straight it does. Look, I wasn't just rowing you out. I thought on it for a good long bit.

It still makes sense for you to go missing. Let it roll for a stretch. Then, later...'

'How later? A month, a year, until I get me pension? Or just until you've done all the earning you can out of Spandrell? It don't sit right, cocker. Not by a long chalk.'

'Look, Bergie. This ain't no way to part. Bitterness. Recrimination. All I want is for you to get away out of it for a bit. Take a rest, some time to think. It's all getting out of hand. Give it time.'

'You sound like a salesman in a clock factory with your time, time, time. I was on my way out of the Smoke as it happens. But the way you been chuntering on makes me suss something's up with you. It just ain't sitting right. I can see the frame, but there's a hole where the picture should be. You get my meaning, Manny?'

Manny spread his hands wide, his chin screwing down into his shoulders. His mouth turned down at the corner and his eyes showed even more white.

'With you,' he said, 'there's always more in what you don't say. You say you're on your way out, but when I say you should do it, you're at me asking what's up.'

'That's me, Manny. Contrary. Comes from being dragged up in a two-up, two-down and one out the back.'

'Wasn't we all? Look, take the money. There's over two grand in the safe. You can even have all the papers from Spanner's club. That's the trust I got. That's an offer to an old friend.'

'No, Manny. There's still arrangements to make. Let me have that shooter you got stashed. Mine went someplace during the bother. I feel a bit starkers without one. I'll be back right soon, maybe tomorrow, and have my cut off you.'

'When tomorrow?'

'Latish. Maybe around eight or nine.'

Manny dropped to his hands and knees to twist out the combination and ease open the safe. He fumbled about among the little leather bags on the top shelf and drew out a canvas bundle. He handed it to me and I undid the drawstrings to let the Webley drop into my palm. It smelled of oil and hemp.

'Better before or after. I got business about that time,' Manny said, spinning the dial and forcing himself to his feet. His voice was casual but tension sang in his throat like a dropped piano.

'Meat lorries, eh?'

Manny smiled slow and sad.

'Like you say, meat lorries. Here.'

He handed me a box of cartridges and I loaded up, keeping the barrel turned away from him. When I looked up his eyes were already on me.

'Do I have to say it?' he asked.

'No,' I said. 'You be careful yourself.'

'Did I get to be seventy by going barefoot through glass?'

The moon dipped behind heavy cloud and I said goodbye in total darkness. The docks were being plastered when I got onto the street, bells rang everywhere.

Eighteen

Bethnal Green station was crowded and I had to queue to get a ticket. A harassed clerk finally punched me one and I went down the escalator behind a lot of mums and grans with armfuls of bedding and kids holding onto their skirts. The air was stale before we got to the bottom.

The platform was filled with people in clutches with their beds laid in the filth and children asleep under the blankets. The odd man in uniform stood around, looking out of it, smoking and staring. There was a cocktail smell of socks, hot bodies and cooking mixed with the dirty-blanket taste the Underground usually had. A sailor sat on his duffle playing a mouth-organ, a song with no words.

I found Doreen half-way down the southbound platform along with her old granny. They were sandwiched between a family of about eight kids and a group of sailors playing cards. She must have looked at me a good long minute before her eyes focussed and she knew me. She didn't say anything. She just got up and picked her way towards me.

'Well,' she said, as if it didn't matter.

'Hello, Dee.'

'How'd you find us?'

'Went knocking at your door. A warden told me you usually crept down here on account of the old lady not trusting the street shelter. He was a bit put out I was out in the street at all.'

'He's like that,' said Dee. 'The old lady wouldn't have none of his rotten shelter with all them old biddies cronied up in the corner with their crates of stout and the swearing. More like a pub than a refuge.'

Her hair straggled as tiredly as her voice. She was hunched inside her coat like a woman three times her age. She wore no make-up and her face looked like washed stone.

'What happened to the country?' I said, looping a stray piece of hair over her ear. 'Thought you was all set to stay down. Then I heard you were back.'

'The old lady again. She'd look out of the window every morning and say "If I have to look at them bloody hills one more day..."'

'And you?'

'Me?' She laughed as though she'd forgotten how. 'I liked it fine. But the old lady ... well, I couldn't leave her to come back alone, could I?'

'I suppose.'

'Well, I couldn't.'

'You look done in, love.'

'You ain't exactly a Greek god y'self. Fighting again?'

'Laundry fell on me.'

'Full of rabbits, I suppose.'

I grinned at her and would have gone on grinning but we were jostled by the people crowding past, searching for a place to settle.

'Like a bloody railway station,' said Dee.

Then we were both laughing and holding on to each other as if we were alone and nothing else mattered. It seemed to last a long time. Finally she pushed me away, looking over her shoulder at the old woman.

'Thanks be,' she said, 'she's finally dropped off. She spent all today sleeping and all last night moaning about being down here. There's no pleasing her.'

'Then don't,' I said. 'Come on, let's get some air, find somewhere we can talk.'

'What?' said Dee up at the roof of the tunnel. 'Up there?'

'There was nothing going on when I was up there last. Maybe they're having a night off. Hitler's orders.'

'All right. But I can't be long.'

'Tell her you had to go to the lav.'

'Don't be crude. Anyway, there ain't one down here. You have to wait until they turn the current off and go in the tunnel.'

We went up the elevator, watching people streaming down the other side.

'They'll have to close it soon if more come down,' said Dee.

The night air was fresher than I'd believed possible as we huddled in the doorway of a sweet-shop. The plate glass was criss-crossed with sticky paper and covered with sold out notices. A copper flashed us with his shielded torch and kept going. Dee giggled, snuggling into my open overcoat.

'Could she get along without you?'

'Who?'

'The old lady. Is she dependent?'

'She'd squeal, but she's capable enough.'

'Then there's no sweat.'

'About what?'

'You and me going off.'

Dee leaned away from me to see my face. She was frowning.

'What's going off when it's at home?'

'You and me. Out of the Smoke for a bit. Month or so, bit of a holiday.'

The laughter had gone when she spoke again.

'Where and why? I don't have to sleep on the pavement to know what's going on in the gutter. Since when have you ever wanted to be anywhere but in this manor?'

'Since now. Get down to Devon or somewhere. Find some fresh air out of all this shit that's flying about.'

'Four legs in a bed, eh?' she said.

'That's part of it.'

'More like all of it.'

'Maybe. You on?'

'Drop the old gran and go off with the one ration book—mine. I'll bet you haven't even got an identity card to call your own. You wouldn't even get to the station without being picked up.'

'Only the best forgeries money can buy, that's all. A pocketful.'

'Let's see.'

She pushed her hand down my shirt front, the fingers stiff as pencils when they touched the gunbutt.

'Oh,' she said, hushed, 'oh.'

'Don't read nothing into that, girl. It's a habit, that.'

She flopped back against the angle where the shop door and the side window met, her head going from side to side.

'No,' she said, 'that's no habit. I never knew you have something you didn't use. Never.'

'That's part of why I want out of here, Dee. After tomorrow, all I'll have inside my coat is my wallet. That's guaranteed.'

'Why not tonight?'

'You what?'

'Go tonight. Why not, if you're serious. Drop that piece of tin in the river and get on a train tonight.'

'Things to do, Dee. Tomorrow's a write-off. First thing the morning after we can catch that train and book ourselves a real clever hotel. Maybe one with more behind the bar than empties.'

'And you'll throw that thing out.'

'You can do it yourself from the train window as we go over Waterloo Bridge. Can't say fairer than that.'

'Throw it now.'

'No way, girl.'

'Now, Bergie, or forget it.'

'Dee.'

'I mean it, Bergie. It's that or me.'

'That's no swop, old love. If I can't oblige, I can't.'

'You saying you can't, or won't?'

'Stay told, Dee. It's this way because it has to be. All the chat in the world won't change it. If I let this go now, I wouldn't make no train. Now or never. I got one night's graft and it's ended. You either want in on the celebrations or you don't. I can't make you, and I ain't begging. So bubble up how you want it. On or off.'

She sank back into the corner so that her face was a smudge in the shadows and her voice could have come from anywhere.

'What does it matter? You've to settle with Laurie Naismith one way or the other. It's been on the cards since you was kids. There's always been feeling there. You don't even know for certain it was him had Ronny taken out. Nor that Spandrell worked you over on his say-so. You was always a lad, Bergie. There's no denying that, but it's only recent you've wanted to use the pointed end of a shooter on someone. This once there's a reason. How long before you don't need one, and you just do it for money?'

'That day won't ever come, and if you knew me better, you'd know it too.'

'Maybe, maybe not.'

'Well, it was a nice thought. Teddah, Dee.'

Something stung my cheek; then again. I hadn't seen her hand move in the darkness. I stood there as she swung her wrist until she couldn't go on; just sobbing in the blackness. It was the first time I'd wanted a smoke since the laundry.

'Waterworks don't work, Doreen. If you change your mind I'll be at the station around eight. Don't be late. I'll not fancy lining up twice for tickets,' I said into the back of her head before walking away. The wire gates were across the entrance to Bethnal Green station when I passed. A copper stood before an easel sign that said

STATION FULL on it. He gave me a light for my cigarette off the end of his.

'What about the regulations?' I said.

He pointed at the sky to the east and snorted. The glow was bright orange.

'If they can't see where to go from that,' he said, 'our fags won't help them.'

I said thanks and walked off towards the glow. I could fancy I felt the heat of the fires on my face. Doreen caught me up before I'd gone more than a hundred yards.

'Well,' she spat, looping her arm through mine, 'I couldn't get back down onto the platform. That rotten jack wouldn't let me through.'

'And nobody loves you, that it?'

'That goes both ways.'

We skirted a roped-off area in the road where a bomb had made a deep scar in the tar blocks. A couple of listless blokes in tin hats were shovelling rubble into it. The scrape of their shovels set my teeth on edge. Glass crunched under our feet.

'Where you going now?' I said.

'Home, maybe.'

'I'll walk you there.'

'And then you'll walk off.'

'I reckon.'

'To do what?'

'Nothing.'

'Why don't you come back home with me? I could cook you up something. There's not much. A bit of bacon and some cocoa.'

'Sounds all right.'

I was suddenly hungry. I was surprised until I realised I hadn't had a bite in twenty-four hours.

I woke up with a start. It was a while before I realised where I was. The dawn was strengthening into day through a chink in the blackout behind the teddy bear's head as he sat lopsided on Doreen's dressing table. Talcum powder dusted the top of his head like dandruff. I was still in the easy chair where I'd sat talking to Dee, the greasy plate on the lino by my foot. My head felt like it had been concreted on at the wrong angle. I got up and tried stretching away the stiffness. Sleeping upright never agreed with me.

The bed was made up and there was a note on the pillow. The whole house felt empty. I unfolded the note and read it.

Bergie,

I've gone to collect gran. I've taken the piece of tin. I'll bury it somewhere it can't be found. It's for the best.

Dee.

I swore at the bear and he looked back with his head on one side, his eyes unfocussed glass. I swore again without putting any expression on his face. When I hit him he sailed into the wall and flopped down behind the bed, one leg showing above the counterpane.

I had the cab drop me on the corner of King's Cross station and I walked through the tunnel across to Argyle Square. There was a light drizzle and the early morning workers weren't hanging around. Everybody seemed to be moving with great purpose.

I had to bang for a long while before anybody moved in the passage. There was a lot of stumbling and muttering before the door opened. It swung inwards with Dotty hanging onto it. Her hair had fallen down around her face like coils of orange rope and her eyes had sunk back into her face. Only one side of her mouth had lipstick on it, a smear of it ran along her cheek. She was drunk.

I got my hand over her mouth just as recognition squirmed in her eyes, cutting off her yell before it was half-way up her throat. She let go of the door to claw at me and her legs gave out from under her. I kicked the door closed and bundled her down into her museum of a parlour. She fell into her chair when I let her and stayed quiet as I pulled her bag from under the table and out of her reach. She watched me sit in the chair facing her using only her eyes, everything else seemed out of control.

'Ernie,' she said. She looked waxier and more unreal than she ever had. The room was bitter with smoke and gin fumes. The city of portraits on the piano had been disturbed and most of them were flat on their backs. Max Miller was on the floor with his glass broken.

'Ernie, where's...'

I emptied the best part of a bottle of Booth's into her glass and put it into her hand. She held onto it as though it were the rail at the top of a long dark flight of stairs.

'Ernie's dead,' I said.

She looked at me as though she had never seen me before.

'That's right,' I added. 'Dead.'

She seemed to notice the glass for the first time. She took half of it down in one jerk. She shuddered without moving anything.

'And then there were three,' she said.

I didn't say anything.

'Cliff, and Dotty, and bastard Bergman.'

'That's right.'

'Bastard,' she said in a conversational way. I picked up her bag and took out her gun. It was covered in fluff and smelled of lipstick. It had a full clip and the bore was clean. I dropped it into my pocket.

'For what it's worth, I'm sorry,' I said.

Dotty scrubbed at her nose with the back of her hand. It took all her concentration.

'I don't care, bastard,' she said into her lap.

I went through her sideboard drawers without taking much care about where things fell. They were full of photographs and old programmes, now and again a list of banknote numbers, but mostly junk. At the back of the cupboard I found a box of forty-five shells with the seals intact. I sat down on the chair again and reloaded the Colt.

'I'm borrowing this,' I said.

'I don't care.'

'Then don't.'

Dotty shrugged and gin went down her dress. She let it soak in.

'I'm off then,' I said.

She shrugged again.

'I hope they kill you,' she said in the way you usually talk about the weather. She stuck her nose down into her glass and tilted it back as far as it would go. This time she didn't spill anything.

I found an empty booth in the station and after dropping my pennies and dialling I got Cliff on the line. I pressed button A and said:

'As far as anybody who's listening is concerned, this is Charlie, right?'

'Yessir, Charlie. What can I do for you?'

'A lot as it happens. You know about the laundry?'

'Yeah.'

'What you don't know is who got it there. Ernie lost out, along with Poncer and the other faces. I dunno how. I wasn't too straight about what was going on. Still ain't.'

'I didn't know,' said Cliff. 'Bad.'

'I need some wheels, Cliff.'

'On the cards.'

'A sherbert. That's the only kind that can really move without bother.'

'A taxi to go to Floral Street. Right, Charlie. Have it there in an hour.'

'That where you'll leave it?'

'That's it.'

'I'll settle with you soon. All right?'
'Settle the other business first. Then get to mine.'
'Ta, Cliff.'
'Nothing,' he said, and rang off.

Nineteen

The drizzle turned to rain, the rain into a downpour. Dollies danced in the streets and people scuttled about like wet crabs. I sat watching the cab from a clear circle in the steamed window of The Ship's public bar. It stood at the kerb getting wetter and shinier the longer it was ignored by the passers-by. I ordered another pint and let the governor bring it across to me. Both of us stared out into the wet dusk. He didn't say anything and neither did I. After a bit he sighed, took the right money from the heap of silver at my elbow and went back behind the bar.

I sipped the beer and it was as wet as the rain and about as tasteless. I drank it down anyway. I shrugged into my overcoat, put on my damp trilby, scooped my change into my pocket, hefted my brown paper parcel and with a nod to the governor went outside. With me gone he'd lost all his trade. He was in the middle of another sigh as the door hit the jamb.

I walked across to the cab and looked through at the rear seat. There was nothing on it but upholstery and nothing on the floor but ribbed rubber. The driving seat was just as empty. I left the glove over the flag and used the key in the dash to start her. She fired first time. I put her into gear and drove out of Floral Street into Whitechapel High Street and turned west. The rain came down harder.

I got to Camden Town in minutes flat. There was no traffic to speak of and only the odd pedestrian. The rank by the island toilets was empty. I got out without locking up. The telephone bell was ringing when I walked past it. I lifted the receiver and left it dangling on its wire. The anti-aircraft guns were quiet and the night was free of droning engines.

I crossed into Bayham Street taking note of the numbers. On the door that I wanted was a bell marked *Allison* and I leaned on it. I must have burned up most of the battery before he fumbled the door open.

He was half-way along the hall with his arm up his back before he knew what was happening. I held him up against the banister rail and let him sweat for a bit.

'You know who I am?' I said into his ear. 'Bergman, remember?'

He nodded, breathing toothpaste against the side of my face.

'Upstairs, then, to your room for a little chat.'

We went up three flights and across a narrow landing. He closed the door behind us and clicked on the light. It was a small room. Bachelor bare, if you know what I mean. There was a rumpled day-bed in the corner beside a curtained recess. His clothes hung there, a suit, a jacket and a couple of pairs of trousers; a suitcase on the floor that was pigskin under the scars. A pair of black shoes that needed cleaning, and a pair of tan oxfords. Under the blacked-out window was a chest of drawers and a small desk with an old Imperial on it. There was also a pipe in a rack and a pouch of tobacco. I pulled a chair out from under the desk and sat astride it with my elbows on the back-rest. Allison lowered himself onto the bed in a squeal of springs.

He looked slighter and younger in his pyjamas and robe, unshaven in a peach-fuzz sort of way, his hands working nervously. I lit up a cigarette one-handed, blew round it to kill the match, and threw the match on the floor. The floor wasn't dirty enough for the dirt to shout at you. Allison looked down at the match with reproach in his eyes. He looked down and kept looking down. I watched him looking down. Finally he knelt forward to pick up the match. I put my foot on the back of his hand. His eyes came up and I closed them with a stream of smoke. I didn't move my foot.

'You're in Carey Street,' I said. 'They're coming for you. Wouldn't be surprised if they ain't on their way now.'

Allison blinked, shook his head, looked at his hand under my shoe and blinked again. His mouth stayed shut.

'True, that. I'm doing you a favour coming here. A big favour since they want me more than they want you. That's what you were all about. They set a rabbit to catch a fox. The fox has got a full belly and a sense of humour. So, he lets the rabbit follow him about until he finds out where the rabbit's burrow is. Then the fox gets angry. You know why?'

Allison didn't ask why. I put pressure on my foot.

'Know why, do you?'

'All right,' said Allison through set teeth, 'why?'

'I knew you'd be interested. I could see right off you were a fellow that was interested in other people. Saw it right off.'

I took time out to take a long draw on my cigarette.

'See, they figured that I'd come after you here. Find out what you was all about. I'd have a chat and find out that you knew nothing. I'd sit here puzzling and they could come right in and have me away as sweet as you please. See what I mean?'

Allison was ready for his cue this time.

'No,' he said, 'I don't see what you mean.'

'It's simple. I didn't do like they planned. I caught up with you on the Underground. I didn't bother with coming here. We had our little chat. They'd figured that they only had to stake out one drum instead of tying up most of their runners all over London. Now d'you see?'

'No,' said Allison with his head on the move again. 'No, I don't, I bloody don't. Anyway, if they're waiting for you here as you say, why have you come?'

'I hate disappointing people. Not in my nature.'

'You're barmy. Bloody insane.'

'That could be right, old son. But it don't sit right having you say so.'

Allison's head dropped between his shoulders, his face close to my shoe. The fingers of his free hand were clenching and unclenching.

'I meant nothing by it,' he said.

'No offence. No, I'm just unpredictable. See, they helped to kill a mate of mine the other night. A little bloke called Ernie. Ugly little bastard with more spark than sense. Well, you met him. So you'd know.'

'I remember.'

I patted Allison's head with the heel of my palm.

'Pays to have a good memory in your game, divorce and that. Well, anyway, back to me and you. I'm here and you're here. I'm the trapped fox in your burrow.'

'Look, I don't see why you say all this. It's stupid.'

'Oh, yeah.'

'People don't go round killing other people, just like that.'

'They don't.'

'You must know it yourself.'

Allison was past sweating and trembling, he was changing-colour scared. I took more smoke down and ash hit the floor beside his hand. I said:

'Oh yes they do. This mob does it the way you and me break eggs. Only they don't save the yolk. Just smash it and leave it lie.'

Allison was looking at his hand again. I lifted my foot and let him have it back. He inched back onto his bed and tucked his fingers inside his pyjama jacket. We listened to the traffic that wasn't passing by and the aeroplanes that weren't flying overhead. Nobody pounded up the stairs or smashed open the door. We could have been miles underground for all the noise and light that was coming through the blackout. If Allison had owned a clock its tick would have been very loud.

'What happens now?' asked Allison. 'I mean, what are you going to do?'

'Me?' I said.

'Yes.'

'Not anything worthwhile. Where's your phone?'

'I use next door's.'

'You what?'

Allison looked apologetic.

'They're out at work all day long. They let me use their place. I use the front room as an office, sort of. I have my letters come here, though. On account of them being on the confidential side.'

I could have sworn. I could have spat, chewed the carpet or just jumped out of the window onto my head. Instead I said:

'Get dressed.'

He let his face go blank.

'That's right, get your knickers on. While you're doing that I'll tell you my little proposition.'

He raked around in drawers and under the bed, putting on a pair of socks in a hurry, as though the sight of his naked feet might give me ideas of the wrong sort. As he hustled into his shirt I dropped a block of fivers on the floor. He froze with only half his face showing over the collar. I could see I had his entire attention.

'If you come up golden on what I want you to do, that roll's yours. With another hundred to follow. Enough to lose you anywhere in the country for a long stretch. If you do it right—to the letter.'

Allison's head came out of the top of his shirt. He had managed to get most of both arms up one sleeve. He looked like all his blood had run out of his navel.

'How much?'

'Two, maybe three hundred. That's a year's wages for most.'

He did a sum in his head and nodded. Somehow he got the shirt on right and buttoned it. His fingers seemed to have a life of their own. He did better with his trousers. They swished up his legs.

'What do I do?'

I took the brown paper parcel from out of my overcoat and dropped it beside the money.

'You deliver that if I don't collect it from you by ten o'clock tomorrow morning.'

'Why am I dressing, then?'

'You take the parcel and all you can get into one suitcase and stay lost until then. Then you go to Waterloo Station. I'll see you there. If I don't come by half-past, you deliver that.'

'Where to?'

'There's a name and an address on it.'

'All right. What then?'

'You go away as far as you can.'

'I've got a married sister in Bristol.'

'So why tell me? I'm the last to know.'

'Yes,' said Allison, 'yes.' He was holding his shoes as though he were displaying them to a customer.

'Show me a pair in brown,' I said.

'What?'

'Hurry up.'

'Yes. Right away.'

'And pack everything in your suitcase. You won't be coming back.'

The street was as dark as it had been before; no lights, no noise and no traffic. The rain was a bit lighter, but not enough to matter. I went down the steps ahead of Allison and let him pull the street door to. His suitcase banged against the railings. Nobody called out, flashed a torch or threw anything. We walked to the cab rank without hurry.

The cab still stood where I had left it. The rank telephone still dangled on the end of its cord. I pointed it out to Allison and told him to hang it up. He dropped his suitcase and laid his overcoat over it. I left him there, crossed to the island and watched the cab through the railings. Allison managed to get the receiver on the hook and did a lot of fumbling to get the door of the box closed. Then he threw his overcoat over his shoulder, hefted the suitcase across his chest and crossed over to the cab. He dropped a hand from the case to open the passenger door. There was a harsh crack and the interior of the cab lit up as bright as day. Allison flew out of vision and I heard his suitcase hit the road.

Everything slowed down. I reached out for the passenger handle on my side and opened the door. It seemed to take for ever for it to open wide enough to see inside. The crouching man with his back to me was rising up, half-turning. His right arm was out as far as it would go, bearing down where Allison had fallen. The Smith and Wesson looked like a toy in his hand.

I went into him with my shoulder, all my weight catching him just above the buttocks. There was a dull thud as his forehead smacked against the roof of the cab. Then he was falling out of the door with his spine arched and his arms wide. There was a handclap as his face hit the ground and his gun skittered away. His legs flailed, kicked, then flopped across Allison. He was still and quiet when I used my foot to turn him over. There was a cut along the lower edge of his hairline; a red octopus of blood running down into his eyes. It didn't stop me from recognising him. He seemed to have a real close feeling for taxis. He'd used one to run Ronny into the ground all those months back in King's Cross. I don't know what I'd expected to feel when I finally caught up with him. I felt as flat as a warmed-up soufflé.

I called Allison's name and after a bit he answered. He said:

'I hit my head.'

He got out from under the bloke's legs and made it to his feet. He brushed his jacket and felt his chest. Then he rubbed the back of his head. That was when he winced.

'Say thank you to your suitcase,' I said.

There was a hole in the pigskin the size of a florin. Allison started making flustered noises. I cut him off.

'You know him?'

He looked down at the bloke on the ground and made a face and nodded.

'He was one of the ones that came to see me all those times. You know, who asked me to follow you.'

'Fair enough. Go through his pockets. Do it without getting between me and him.'

He came up with a wallet with letters and money inside, a key-ring and a small crucifix, a handful of shells, small change and a wrist-watch. I took them from him as he fished them out.

'That's all,' he said when he'd finished.

'Right,' I said, 'get his legs.'

Between us we hefted the bloke into the back of the cab and kneeled him up with his head on the seat. I found some rope under the driving seat and tied his hands to his feet, with another loop running around his throat and down around his ankles. Allison watched me with his eyes wide.

'If he tries to stand up he'll choke himself,' he said.

'That's right.'

'But he could kill himself.'

'Save me then, won't it.'

'But...' said Allison.

'Well?'

Allison just looked at me.

'Look, sunshine,' I said, 'he did his best to put a hole

in your supper, and mine if he'd had a chance. Sorry is for the storybooks.'

There was nothing he could say. He just stood there.

'Teddah,' I said.

'Yes,' he said, waiting.

'What are you waiting for, a bloody Bradshaw? Get off out of it. I don't want to see you until tomorrow, right?'

'No,' he said. 'I mean yes.'

I climbed into the cab and started her up. Allison picked up his wet suitcase and went off towards the Underground without looking back. He looked like somebody's eldest son going on his holidays.

I knuckled Manny's front door and waited. Nothing happened. I knocked again. A radio was making noises towards the back of the house; the buzz of a stand-up comic and a laughing audience. I turned the doorknob to see what would happen and the door opened. I stepped through and closed it behind me. All I could hear was the radio and my own breathing. I couldn't see anything. There was a smell in the air; something added to the damp and the smell of old cooking. Sharper and more recent. I turned on the light.

The passage was much as it always was. The same dust on the floor, the same stained paper, the same lino. The door to the front room was ajar. I looked through the crack between the door and the jamb at the back of a head and part of an ear. There were spots on the neck and the collar wasn't clean.

'Come out of it,' I said.

The neck stiffened and moved out of sight.

'Then I come in. You want that?' I said, and cocked the Colt. It made a noise like a damper being moved in an old grate. There was a pause, then:

'All right.'

I stood back and watched him come out. He was tall, young, even spottier from the front, and scared. He was wearing overalls and heavy boots. It was the kid from Cliff's garage, only this time he wasn't chewing gum.

'What's your game then, Sidney?' I said. It was all I could think of.

'Nothing,' he said, 'straight.'

I looked at him. He tried looking back but it didn't come off. He looked at everything but me. His hair had collapsed into wet spears across his forehead and there were wet circles around his armpits. The acne on his face looked painted on.

'Where's Manny?' I asked.

He didn't answer straight off.

'In there,' he said finally. With an effort he managed to point towards the back room.

'Alone,' I said.

'Oh, yeah.' Something like a laugh came out of his throat. 'He's alone all right. Yeah.'

'Show me.'

'No. I don't ... look, I don't. You can't make me go in there.'

He backed away from me with his hand out. He hit the arm of the overstuffed chair and fell into it.

'I went,' he said. 'I ain't again.'

He pulled his knees up in a foetal curl and wrapped his arms around his head. I pulled the door shut and turned the key. He wasn't going anywhere.

The back room was a shambles. The furniture had been slashed and the stuffing pulled out. All the drawers from the sideboard had been up-ended and the contents raked through. The table was overturned with Manny's teapot and glass underneath it in pieces. The safe was open and empty.

One chair was upright. Manny sat in it cross-legged, a dressing gown over his fair-isle pullover and slacks. His hair was slightly ruffled and he was smiling his sad smile at the wall. One of his slippers had fallen off.

There was a thin red line at one end of his smile and a red circle in the middle of his chest.

The added smell was thick in the room. The smell of cordite. Manny had gone on the longest journey he would ever take.

I turned off the laughing radio and let Manny smile at me in the quiet. I found a chair in the rubble, set it up facing him and sat on it. I sat there a long time. Then I put his slipper back on his foot and let myself out.

Sid was where I had left him, still curled up with his face buried. Behind the door where he had been standing was a holdall, tight-zippered and bulging. I opened it up and had a look through. Most of it was junk. Manny's junk.

There was a clock from his sideboard, a statuette of a nymph with a chip in the stand, a watch with the strap missing, a canteen of hall-marked cutlery and a paper bundle.

I opened the bundle and looked down at a fat slab of white fivers with my name on the band. The piece of paper was a list of addresses with amounts of money alongside. I had been to all of them and made collections.

I picked up the nymph and hit the boy across the knee with it. He sat upright and looked at me with his eyes all the way open.

'You thieving toerag,' I said in a voice I didn't recognise. 'I'm gonna leave you in pieces. Scared of a dead man, but not enough so you couldn't nick his gear with him sitting there watching you.'

'I didn't mean nothing. He was dead. He didn't need it. I just thought it'd go to waste. I didn't mean nothing by it.'

'Shut up.'

He shut up.

'Now you tell me what you were here for if it wasn't to row old Manny out of a clock and a few bob.'

'I didn't do him. He was like that when I come. Straight he was.'

'I'm listening, but I don't hear anything I like.'

'Cliff said I was to come here with a message. I had to drop everything and get round here. I come and there wasn't no answer, so I come in. And there he was.'

'What message?'

'A note I had to give him. Cliff wouldn't use the phone on account of there was too many around ear-wigging.'

'Where is it?'

'What?'

I used the nymph again.

'The note, burke.'

He fumbled inside his overalls and handed me a scruffy square of off-white paper. It said:

Manny,
    it's a con. they want you alone to turn you over. Cliff.

I held my lighter under the note and turned the wheel with my thumb. It crisped and was gone. The boy was looking at me like I was a mongoose.

'Who was at the garage when you left?'

'Cliff, like. Laurie, and that Jacko. They was there.'

'That all?'

'Yeah. That Mister Spandrell was like there for a bit. He give Cliff a coating, and he wouldn't even answer Laurie when he said anything. Just looked at him funny. I was glad to come away out of it.'

'Don't get too glad.'

'But Cliff said I could slope off.'

I speared him in the chest with the nymph's arms and held him against the back of the chair.

'You'll do what I tell you. Get it?'

'I got it. All right, I got it,' he whined. A little spark showed at the back of his eyes, gone almost before it arrived.

'Too right you will,' I said. 'Now, pick up the phone

and call the garage. Ask for Cliff. When he's on, you hand it to me. Say anything I don't like and you know what'll happen.'

'I know.'

He dialled, listened, then spoke.

'Hello, this is Sid. Oh, hello Mister Naismith. Can I have a word with Cliff? Yeah? Ta.'

I took the receiver out of his hand and held it to my ear, my eyes on Sid. Sid looked at the nymph. I twirled it just to watch his eyes revolve.

'Yeah,' said Cliff.

'It ain't Sid, Cliff.'

'No, it ain't.'

'You were too late for Manny,' I said. 'Way too late.'

'That's bad. You better lie in in the morning if you got a cold that bad.'

'They put a bullet right through him. Just the one in the right place. I'm coming over. I don't want you in this. Stay dry. I'm losing too many mates the way things are moving. I know Laurie and Jacko are there, and I reckon Spandrell's expected. Any more?'

'Three or four on the wagons. I can handle it. You get over to your mother. She'll tuck you up fine. I wouldn't have you taking on all that work on your own.'

'No other way, keep your barnet down. Teddah.'

I rang off before he could say any more. Sid made as if to stand up. I slammed him back, hard.

'You ain't through yet, son. Not by a mile.'

'But Cliff said I could get off home.'

'You,' I said, 'are staying right here. You know what a *vacha* is?'

He shook his head. I tapped his chest with the nymph.

'That's you. A night vigil for the dead. And you're it.'

Twenty

The front of the garage looked like a deserted amusement park that had lost its eccentric lettering and managed somehow to be made of concrete. It loomed in the rain, shuttered and dark, the three pumps out front like tin sentinels; the aerodrome doors closed and as glossy as only rain-wet paint can be.

I was crouched behind a row of drums near the forecourt entrance being grinned at by an enamelled cut-out man with a notice across his chest that said SORRY NO PETROL. He didn't look sorry at all.

Something coughed a street away; coughed and whined into a lower gear. A shadow droned into the end of the street, throwing spume from its tyres and thin beams from its louvred lamps. Another lorry turned in behind it.

I banged some life into my legs and readied myself to jump. The aerodrome doors grated open behind me as the first lorry turned into the forecourt and ran straight into the garage. The second turned in almost immediately afterwards. I came out from behind the drums and jumped for the tailboard. My foot caught in the iron rail above the mudguard as I grabbed at the locking bar. I got it in one and hung on. I was swept past the pumps and into the darkened garage.

The doors started running together. Using the door hinges as hand- and foot-holds I got up to the roof of the lorry and rolled onto it just as the doors clanged together and the lights came on. There was a scrape and a drum-roll as the bar was dropped into place.

Greetings were called as the cab doors were slid back, followed by the peck of feet dropping onto concrete.

'All right then?'

'Cakewalk except for the rain. Poxy stuff cost us a good hour.'

'I tell you, you need a long memory to find your way about them country lanes. There ain't a signpost for bleeding miles.'

'Leave it out. You gotta graft to earn, ain't you?'

'Who's bellyaching? I'm only saying, ain't I?'

'That's only starters for you. Here, have a snout and stow it for your grandkids.'

There was spasmodic laughter then, as though they were coughing out the tension. I rolled over on my back and looked up into the metal rafters, a jigsaw of cross-hatching shadows, close enough to touch without standing up. I rolled back and inched over to the side of the roof and peered down.

There were six men in a group by the cab of the first lorry. Laurie was leaning his elbow on his knee, his foot on the lorry's bumper. He looked as relaxed as a fisherman with a full bag. Jacko stood behind him with a straight face and his hands deep inside his overcoat pockets. Only his eyes seemed alive.

The others were new to me; probably contract drivers earning by the run. I couldn't see Cliff anywhere. The office door was closed.

'Where this little lot go, then, Mister Naismith?' asked one of the drivers. 'The usual down in the Garden?'

'No,' said Laurie, 'been a bit of an upset.'

'Oh, blimey,' said the driver. 'We ain't rowed out, are we? I wanna get home for some cocoa and grumble.'

'You'll get it, Quill, soon enough.'

'Who's rowed us out, then? Not that Manny,' said Quill.

'That's nothing to you, Quill,' said Laurie. 'This end's none of yours.' He took a cigarette out of a gold case and let one of the drivers light it for him.

'Quill don't mean nothing by it,' said the driver with the matches. 'It's just you can't help but pick up the odd bubble. He ain't one to nose.'

'Right,' agreed Quill, 'all we want is the poppy. The lads have been gutting and skinning from Sevenoaks to here. They just wanna get off out of it.'

Laurie let smoke plume out through his smile as he dropped a hand on Quill's shoulder.

'Nobody's bitching. Manny has blown us out, as it happens. Can't raise him on the blower. You take this lot off down to the wharf. It'll have to store for a bit.'

'What about the gates?'

'Taken care of. It's expected.'

'Fair enough. Who coughs the sovs?'

'Right here as usual,' said Laurie. He reached inside his coat and pulled out a roll of notes, peeling them off into Quill's palm. Quill's lips moved as he counted.

'Right,' he said. 'Ta, Mister Naismith. I'll divi up with the lads when we're through the gates. See you about, then.'

'You'll hear from me. Jacko'll go with you to see it goes smooth.'

'Don't trust us, eh?' laughed Quill, climbing up into the cab. Laurie slapped him on the back.

'No,' he said, 'not as far as I could spit you.'

Jacko walked round to climb in the other side of Quill's lorry and the others crammed into the front of the one I was lying on. The motors growled awake almost together. I kneeled up and stepped up onto the nearest girder as the lights died. The lorries rolled out from under me and went off into the night. I inched my way along the stanchion bars to the wall and hung there as Laurie closed the doors and put on the lights. When he'd fixed the bar he leaned against the metal and shook with silent laughter, his head right back and his tonsils showing. He laughed for a long time.

As long as it took him to see me. He didn't stop all of a sudden like I expected, he just ran down as if he'd laughed all he wanted.

I dropped to the ground with the Colt out in front of me.

'Well, Bergie,' he said. 'It didn't take you long to get here.'

I didn't say anything.

'Not talking, eh?' He dropped his dog-end to the floor and started to reach inside his jacket.

'Leave it out,' I said.

He shrugged.

'Whatever you say.'

I jerked the Colt at the office and said: 'In there. Straight in, with your hands where I can see them.'

'After you,' he offered. The smile on his face was as permanent as a wave in a thirty-bob hairdo.

'Come on.'

He smiled down at the Colt and sauntered across to the office. At the door he hesitated slightly, working his shoulders under his coat. I stabbed him in the spine with the barrel and pushed him. The door banged open and he sprawled in. I stepped straight in behind him and, pressing the gun down into the back of his neck, looked straight into the face of the man behind the desk; sitting all the way down in the chair and looking back. Neither of us smiled.

'Well,' he said. 'Laurie said you'd make it. Cost me a fiver.'

He was dressed much as always. Blue shirt, black tie, dark blue suit and a matching raincoat. His trilby was on the back of his head. He was toying with a cigarette and a gold lighter.

'Detective Sergeant Barrett,' I said. 'The terror of the tarts. A wonder you can afford it on a copper's pay. But then, you don't, do you?'

He inclined his head and looked watchful. The sides

of his face were blotchy where his beard grew, as though he'd struggled through a shave with a dull blade. The rest of his face was the high pink of a man that spent a lot of time out and about. He looked very clean. He revolved the lighter between his fingers so that light gleamed on the little facets of its checkered face.

'It's going to be a pleasure being the arresting officer,' he said. 'It'll mean a feather in mine. There's a man at the Yard that's really interested in having you in for chats.'

'I'll give you one thing, Barrett,' I said, 'you've got a lot of face. Get up, Laurie. Make yourself comfortable by your friend.'

When he was sat down I said: 'Where's Cliff?'

Barrett's eyes hardly moved. They flicked down into the corner behind the desk.

'Who's Cliff?' he said.

I reacted without thinking. The Colt swept in a short arc across his chin, knocking him right out of his chair. He fell half across Laurie's lap before rolling onto the floor with his head against the wall. The chair ran a short way on its castors and stopped as it hit something soft. I hoisted the desk and smashed it against the wall. Cliff was in a huddle in the corner with a greenish weal down the side of his face. His eyelids were flickering as though he were coming back from a long way away.

'You don't hang about, do you?' I said through frozen lips. 'Don't waste a minute.'

'He's all right,' said Laurie. 'Just a few lumps. He was lucky, mind.'

'I'll give you lucky.'

'He shouldn't have tried it on. Outclassed he was. Like you are now.'

'Like Manny was, eh, Laurie? That must have been real easy.'

'I didn't sweat it,' he said. 'Do it simple, do it neat.'

'And the road's clear for Spanner to take a long walk,

that it? Leave you fat on the top of the pile. That's if you can trust your friend here.'

'Spanner?' smiled Laurie. 'I reckon he's about done for.'

'By a face with a shooter that hangs about Camden Town a lot,' I said.

'Something like that.'

I nodded and said: 'Sounds very neat. Barrett whistles up a vanload of the boys in blue and has me away to the big nick. Along with all those papers out of Manny's safe. Well, maybe not all, only the ones that don't rate; and Spanner's found with a gun in his hand and a big hole in his head. Maybe even a note by the body. That the sort of thing?'

Neither of them answered. Laurie looked amused and Barrett held his jaw as he gently moved it from side to side.

'You make a lovely couple,' I said. 'But like most marriages there's something that ain't sitting straight. There's enough in them papers to put the whole firm out to grass. Including all the favour merchants. Your name's down there, Barrett, along with amounts and what for. One thing about Spanner, he's a neat book-keeper.'

'Wind,' said Laurie. 'You're farting through your face.'

Barrett's hand stopped running along his jaw. He just held his chin with his eyes on Laurie. Laurie crossed his legs and smoothed his tie.

'He wouldn't be just mouthing, would he?' asked Barrett.

Laurie tucked his tie inside his jacket and brought his thumb and forefinger down his collar.

'Let him talk,' he said. 'That's what he's here for.' He turned to me and smiled. 'That's what you're here for, ain't it, Bergie? Chat time. We both know you ain't got it in you to chop anyone cold. Not in your nature.'

He could have been right. I didn't know either way. I couldn't work out why he was so calm. There wasn't a crack showing anywhere. He was as smooth and smiling as he ever was. Cliff's fingers jerked and spread out on the floor as his elbows rose and his back muscles bunched. He pressed down and pushed himself up in a kneeling position. His eyes were more closed than open.

'Round two, champ,' I said. 'Let's have you on your feet.'

He stayed where he was and let his head hang down between his shoulders. Barrett reached out for the chair and pulled it towards him, using it to get to his feet. I let him flop into it and cuddle his face. He wasn't clean any more. Oil and dust caked one side of his raincoat.

'What about that list, Laurie?' he said, as though his jaw wasn't hinged right. 'That don't sound kosher.'

'Nor it don't, Jack,' smiled Laurie. 'But you can't blame me for wanting a bit of an edge.'

'He'll drop you, soon as it suits,' I said.

Laurie stopped smiling and gave me a hard look.

'I've heard all I want to from you, Bergie. You've been bubbling off for too long. I think we've heard enough out of you.'

'There's more,' I said. 'See, your mate from Camden Town didn't get to Spanner. *I* got to *him*.'

The office went cold and quiet. The strip-light in the ceiling buzzed and Cliff breathed in and out rustily. Then he coughed and used the wall to get to his feet. Nobody looked at him.

'You always was a fly in the ointment,' said Laurie very softly with his head moving from side to side. 'Always was. You wouldn't want to prove that to me now, would you?'

I just looked at him.

'No,' he said. 'I don't suppose you would. Top him, did you?'

'Didn't have to. He came easy,' I said. 'Matter of fact, there wasn't time to breathe in hardly before he rolled over with his paws in the air.'

'Just like that, eh?' sneered Laurie.

'That's it,' I said and dropped the big gold shells onto the floor. 'These fell out of his suit as he rolled over. Badly cut grey job. Even Burton's would baulk at putting a label inside those lapels.' I tutted. 'Shocking.'

Barrett's face was the colour of old cheddar. A nerve was jumping under his right eye. He said: 'That's it for me ... I'm out of it. Do what you like, Laurie. I ain't in this for a pension.' He made as though to stand.

'Sit down!' snapped Laurie. 'This'll take some figuring, that's all. You running off with wet pants won't change nothing.'

I got hold of the telephone from off the floor and let the receiver dangle as I dialled seven digits. Then I held the earpiece against my face and listened to the double burring until somebody said: 'Square Ring.'

'Put me through to the office,' I said.

Laurie's hands smoothed along his thighs and the fingers spread wide before biting into the material.

'Who's this, then?' asked the telephone.

'Tell Spanner it's Cliff's garage.'

'Hang about.'

Barrett touched his mouth with a careful finger without taking his eyes off Laurie. Laurie watched me.

'Office,' said Spanner.

'How did you like my parcel?' I asked him.

'Looks like he fell off the shelf. He's a bit chipped,' said Spanner, as though he had bodies dropped onto his doorstep once a week.

'Sung to you yet? He's got a lovely line of patter once you get him started. I was almost tempted to keep him. But I figured you'd have the more use.'

'Happens I have,' said Spanner without sounding grateful. 'Happens so. And happens you knew there was a couple of bundles out of my safe on him. Nothing heavy, like, nothing that'd get us more than a parking ticket. Shop-window stuff, is it? Just enough to let me know my files have somehow changed hands? That the kind of thing?'

'You're too clever for me by half, Mister Spandrell,' I said. 'You should take that up with young Laurie, shouldn't you? I mean, not really white to talk the firm's business with a stranger.'

'Happens I should. There's a couple of numbers that haven't answered tonight that should have. People that should rightly be home. See my meaning?'

'I see it. Manny's might be one of them.'

'Gone on his holidays, has he?'

'Without leaving his chair,' I said.

Spandrell didn't have an answer for that. He just listened to me breathing for a bit. I said: 'There's a couple of lorries gone missing too. Full of good Kentish mutton. You'll have to change tomorrow's menus.'

'You know a good bit too much, Bergman. I'll have you before the night's out. I'll have my way over any of my firm that's strayed, too. You'll take second place to me in that. Got me?'

'Whatever you say, Mister Spandrell. Why don't you say goodbye to them personal? They're sitting here looking at me, Jack and Laurie. Here.'

I flipped the receiver across to Laurie, then the cradle. He caught them in either hand and kept them well away from his face.

'Cliff,' I said. 'Can you make it out the door? It's time we wasn't here.'

'Stay where you are, you black fart,' said Laurie. 'Nobody's going any place.'

'Teddah, Laurie,' I said. 'I don't reckon to see you again, except as a bit in the stop press.'

'I'll show you,' Laurie said to me, then into the telephone: 'Hello, Spanner. Nothing to sweat over. He's going nowhere with his fairy tales. He's got a handful of deuces against aces.'

I could hear Spandrell's voice across the width of the office. Laurie shot me a look out of a white face. I smiled back. There were cracks showing everywhere now. Even his collar had crooked up over his lapel. After a bit he stopped listening and rang off.

'He didn't buy it,' he said shakily.

'I'll leave you to it, then,' I said. 'You'll be needing all your concentration. Wouldn't want to be in the way. Come on, Cliff.'

'You heard me,' said Laurie. Cliff stayed where he was.

'You and your loyalties,' Laurie spat at me. 'Stick by your mates, never con a pal. All sodding hearts and flowers. Well, I've got a big bubble for you. That shooter you're cuddling ain't worth a cold carrot. Manny conned you on my say so. He gave you a bent shooter to come here with. How's that for a laugh?'

My smile stuck like it was glued on.

'No way,' I said. 'Manny wouldn't have done that to me.'

Cliff looked at me as though he was saying goodbye, and said: 'He did.'

My mouth opened but nothing came out. I coughed and tried again. It didn't work.

Laurie put his hand inside his jacket and drew out a Webley, snapping off the safety and pointing it at me. 'This one, on the other hand, does work. It worked on Manny lovely.'

'Don't do it, Laurie,' I said.

His arm snapped out at me, his finger curling and tightening. The Colt jumped in my hand with a roar and smoke billowed, tasting bitter. Laurie froze as the middle of his tie jumped and grew a hole with frayed edges. He sat up in the chair with his arm straight out in front of him and his face blank.

Barrett said something that nobody understood.

The Webley dropped to the floor. Laurie looked past me as he stood up. He took a step and then another, jerky little steps that looked harder and harder to make. I stood aside and let him claw the door open and make his way out of the office. His heels weren't touching the floor. He tiptoed away making sharp little taps on the concrete. The door closed behind him, bounced away from the jamb, then slowly shuddered closed. The tapping went on for a long time before we couldn't hear it any more.

Barrett leaned down over his shoes. He didn't straighten up. He hung forward over his knees with his wrists curled either side of his feet, gasping at the floor. I took hold of Cliff's arm and led him out.

'You bastard,' Barrett said to the floor. I leaned back inside and said: 'Losing never was much of a cackle. You should have reckoned on there being a chance of it.'

'Smart monkey. Spandrell's got your number. He'll not let you roll under the floorboards again. Not now,' Barrett said without moving.

'You ain't in such clever shape yourself, Barrett. When Spandrell gets your Irish canary singing, he'll have you tied close enough to Laurie to make you twins. 'Course, you could reach down for that Webley under your nose and try doing him a favour.'

For a moment it seemed that he saw merit in the idea, then he took a look at my face and left his hands where they were.

'Pity,' I said. 'That would have made everything neat and lovely. Now Spanner'll be jostling the boys in blue to get to you first. I reckon you'll do better if Spanner gets here first. Leastways it'll be quick. He'll not hang about.'

Barrett came up at me in a lunge with his fingers out. His mouth was open and full of noise. I drove the Colt hard into his middle and crossed to his jaw with a short left. He went down on his clean side and did some more gasping.

'Sorry, cocker,' I said. 'I ain't making it quick for you. Spanner can do all his own topping. Like he says, it's up to the firm to handle its own.'

I used the door to shut him away from sight. I could hear him snuffling through the panelling.

Laurie was slumped up against the aerodrome doors, one arm above his head, the fingers hooked over the bar. He had coughed the last of his life out onto the floor in a dark red puddle. He looked very young, a shrunken boy inside a man's suit. His hand fell into his lap as I worked the bar and let in the night air. It was cold and fresh and smelled very sweet. It had stopped raining.

Cliff looked at me with his very white eyes, still filmed and dazed. He held out his hand. I took it and let him crush my fingers with his long black ones. He said: 'What now?'

I shook my head.

'I dunno. I've got to meet a bloke tomorrow and pick up some papers. And maybe meet a girl.'

'They wouldn't be Spanner's papers, would they?' said Cliff. 'But...'

'You've heard of photocopies, ain't you? Well, that's all Manny had, and that's all Laurie got. Like he said, everybody's got to have an edge.'

'Yeah, you'd better get off. Reckon Spanner'll be getting here soon. He'll not hang about.'

'And you?' I asked.

'Just play it dumb like always. No trick to it.'

'Be lucky.'

'My middle name. Listen, it's good Manny came through. I really reckoned he had filed the pin on that gun.'

'Maybe he did,' I said. I slapped his shoulder and walked away.

Twenty-one

Waterloo was packed with people. Most of the men were in uniform. They stood in rows, lounged against pillars and walls, or sat on kitbags looking at nothing. Allison appeared under the clock as it clicked to five minutes to ten. He still carried his pigskin case and his overcoat. He sat them down and watched me walk towards him. His eyes stuck out of his face like organ-stops. He held the parcel out to me as I stopped in front of him.

'I did it like you said,' he said. 'I've kept on the move all night.'

I pushed the parcel back at him.

'Keep it. Deliver it like I said.'

'But that was if you didn't show.'

'You want another hundred or don't you?'

He licked his lips and nodded. I pulled out some notes and stuffed them into his top pocket.

'Don't just leave it at the desk. You ask to see him personal. You never know, he could put some business your way.'

'Really?'

'What, old Wally Lemmon? One of the best.'

'Straight?'

'Straight,' I said. 'Go on, don't keep him waiting.'

Allison held out his hand and I slapped his palm.

'Go on, hop it.'

He grabbed up his coat and bag and walked off with a jaunty tread. He was soon lost in the swirling crowd. After an hour with Lemmon he'd have earned his money ten times over, maybe more.

'Hello,' said a girl's voice. I turned round and there was Doreen in a new-looking coat and her hair up in a Victory roll. She looked as fresh as newly cut flowers.

'Hello,' I said.

'You could use a shave,' she said.

'Probably.'

'Look,' she said, 'about that gun.' She looked around her in a quick sweep with her hand up to her mouth. 'About that, you know...'

'Forget it,' I said.

'But...'

'Forget it. It's all over. You want to get that train or don't you?'

'Oh, Bergie. I'm so glad. I couldn't sleep or anything.'

'You shouldn't have worried. It all worked out.'

'I knew it would. I just knew...'

I took her arm and steered her towards the platform. 'One day I'll tell you all about it.'

The tannoy suddenly blared and the pigeons took off for their circuit of the rafters. We threaded through the crowds and joined the queue for the ten-fifteen. We shuffled forward with Doreen on my arm, gripping me like I was liable to run off without warning. I patted the back of her hand and said: 'Let go a second. I need that arm to get the tickets.'

She gave me a bright grin and dropped her hands to fiddle with her shoulder bag. She undid the flap and looked into the mirror sewn inside it, her tongue running along her lipstick. I reached inside my jacket for the tickets, my hand brushing against the butt of the Colt. I was thinking about the look on her face when I tossed it out of the carriage window. Then I wasn't smiling any more and I stopped fingering the tickets and gripped the gun.

Doreen was poking at her eyebrows with a forefinger, her eyes creased in concentration in the mirror. I could see the whole of one side of her face, part of her shoulder and some of the crowd behind us. A man was ploughing through the people. He was staring and looked unbalanced. Dirt and oil smeared one side of his raincoat and the right side of his jaw was lumpy and discoloured.

I made a sound and Doreen looked at me sharply, her face full of questions. She said: 'Bergie?'

'Don't look at me Dee,' I told her in a low voice. 'Just go forward with the queue. I'll catch you up in a minute.'

'But...'

'Shut it, Dee. Do as I say.'

Her hand came up to catch at my arm. I pushed her elbow with enough force to spin her half round. Before she could recover I had stepped behind her and walked off the other side of the queue. Somebody shouted. There was a clatter as a suitcase hit the ground. It sounded like somebody had burst through the line behind me. There was another shout. Long and high and wild. I ran.

I got in amongst the crowd, twisting and turning around people and luggage. A long wagon piled with bags and cases loomed in front of me. I jumped at it, trying to clear the top. My torso went over as clear, sharp edges bit at the top of my thighs. I sprawled in the cascading luggage, kicking out to get over the top. I was thrashing about like a landed fish, hooked up and unable to move. With a sudden slide the whole pile came apart and dropped. I hit the floor with my shoulder and bit my tongue. Cases fell all around me. I got up on one knee.

Barrett was pounding forward using everything he had. Banging down his feet in long heavy strides. He had the Webley held in at waist height. He was three jumps away. There was an orange flash and a suitcase jumped off the pile that was left on the wagon.

A porter who had come forward to give me a hand jumped backwards in Olympic style and put his thumbs into his waistcoat pockets. His open mouth looked deep enough to drop stones down and wait for the splash.

Barrett fired again. Sparks splashed along the front bar of the wagon and something whined off into the rafters.

I started running again. The barrier was being swung across one of the platforms just prior to a train pulling out. I reached it before it clanged to, spinning the ticket collector to the floor. I caught the glimpse of other uniforms coming forward as I raced up the platform. The guard's door was still open and he stood just inside, furling his flag. I grabbed the side and heaved myself in, cannoning into him. He sat back into a pile of mail sacks and his breath came out in an *oof*.

There was a lot of shouting on the platform and the sound of many running feet. I took a look. Barrett was running flat out with a couple of station police hard on his heels, an MP close behind them. The train was moving, picking up speed in smooth jerks.

Barrett turned and snapped a shot at the men behind him. They all went down in a rush, one of the railway men spinning with his hand to his chest before he hit the ground.

I ripped open the door on the other side of the van, looking out at the blurring sleepers. The guard started up from the floor to catch at my legs. I kicked him away just as Barrett's face appeared in the opening on the other side. He jumped and held on in the doorway with his eyes full of me.

I drew back from the door and jumped. The track came up at me in a rush of cinders and shining rails. I tumbled over and over, slid and then hammered to a stop against the side of the platform. Everything seemed torn or broken.

Barrett appeared in the doorway of the guard's van. His mouth was working as he spat something at me. I couldn't hear him for the scream of a train letting off steam somewhere behind me. The station policeman and the MP were still running after the train. The gap between them and the last carriage widening visibly.

The rails under my legs were vibrating. I looked along the track as a train bore down on me with squealing brakes. I got up and hoisted myself onto the platform.

Barrett jumped then. Like me, he hit the track in a roll, slid and stopped. He was up on his feet sooner than I'd managed, staggering towards me. The gun miraculously still in his hand. He stopped, gripped it in both hands and sighted at me.

The train hit him. One minute he was there and then the train was rolling past me with the faces at all the windows, doors banging open and people leaning out to watch for the moment that they could get off.

Then they were all around me. Hurrying for the barrier and patting their pockets for tickets. I put my hand up to my face and it came away wet and streaked. People jostled me from all sides, knocking me first one way, then the other.

I stumbled along in the stream towards the barrier on rubbery legs, only the crowd's density keeping me upright. A pillar came up past me and I grabbed hold of it. The crowd separated and went around me.

There was a waste bin clamped to the pillar, half-filled with paper. I drew out the Colt and buried it as far down as it would go. Nobody clapped me on the shoulder or even looked at me. I let go of the pillar and went with the crowd.

Through the coach windows I could see a lot of people milling around on the opposite platform and looking down under the wheels at the spot where Barrett had disappeared. Maybe they thought we'd both gone under.

I kept walking, teasing a fiver off my roll. I held it out to the collector and said:

'All the way. I can't find my ticket anywhere. Must have dropped it.'

He gave me change and I was through. My head pounded as I stumbled to where I'd left Doreen. The queue seemed to be made of a line of jelly that rippled across a series of small hills. I struck off at an angle and came up behind it as if I were a late arrival, looking for the back of her head.

I missed it and she grabbed my arm from behind, pulling me in beside her.

'Hello, darling,' she said brightly. 'I thought you weren't going to make it. You look as if you've been running.'

She made a lot of other chatter about how dishevelled I looked as she wiped my face with her handkerchief, straightened my tie and generally cleaned me up. She got the tickets from out of my inside pocket, got them clipped at the barrier, and then we were through and walking up the station and into our reserved seats. We had the carriage to ourselves when the train pulled out. That was when the tone of her chatter changed and she tore into me. I don't think she stopped talking for an hour.

Twenty-two

The last of the autumn sun was shafting down through the mean houses onto the rubble of the bombed site. Weeds stood in clumps, browned and past death, amongst the bricks and cans and springs.

Doreen pointed a listless hand off to a mound of debris a little higher than the other mounds.

'I hid it under there,' she said.

I walked across what had been a front door step and down into a depression that was the two front rooms. Dust kicked up from my shoes and ran off behind me in a grey plume.

I reached what had been the rear fence and walked along it to the far corner where an old cistern lay on its side, rusted and holed, a mattress draped over it. I kneeled up on it and thrust my hand down behind it, between its bottom and the fence. After a bit of groping my fingers brushed against a piece of waterproof cloth wrapped around something hard. I got a good grip on one corner and pulled it out. It came up easily, showering fine dust over my trousers. With infinite care I separated the folds and looked down at Manny's Webley. It gleamed dully and shot a highlight into my eyes as I turned it in my hand.

The street was empty but for Doreen. A cat jumped onto the fence and gave me a golden stare of disdain. He sat on the top of an upright cleaning his bib and took no notice when I put a can up on the fence about six feet from him. His fur was more important.

I stepped back and clicked off the safety, sighted and

pulled the trigger. The can jumped high, rolled in the air and clattered down into the next garden. The cat just wasn't there any more.

When I crunched back the way I'd come the dust clouded ahead of me. I didn't see it. I was too busy saying goodbye to an old friend.